THE WRONG PRINCE CHARMING

HOLLY RENEE

The Wrong Prince Charming

This is a work of fiction. Names, places, characters, and incidents are the product of the author's imagination and are used fictitiously.

Visit my website at www.authorhollyrenee.com.

Cover Design: Regina Wamba

Editing: Ellie McLove of My Brother's Editor and Becca Hensley Mysoor of Edits in Blue

Proofreading: Judy Zweifel

Stay notified of new releases, sales, and monthly newsletters:

www.authorhollyrenee.com/subscribe

To my incredibly hot husband.
Never let them doubt that I get all my inspiration from you.

The ultimate book boyfriend. ;)

CHAPTER 1

I'D NEVER BEEN to one of the Kappa's legendary parties. I'd heard about them, of course. Within the first three minutes of my campus tour, someone was already talking about them.

Theo had told me a little about them too, but I didn't get all the dirty details until I met my new dormmate, Dillon. She had the low down on everything.

And I mean everything.

But experiencing it firsthand was completely different from hearing about it.

When we stepped into the house, it was clear that Kappa parties were the party to be at. It was only ten PM, and there were already people *everywhere.*

The frat house was huge and looked like the only time a girl was in this house was for parties or when someone was getting laid, because there wasn't a feminine touch anywhere to be seen. A TV bigger than any I had ever seen before covered one wall and had some sports talk show on even though you couldn't hear a word of what they were saying over the booming music.

Dillon tugged on my hand to pull me through the crowd that was attempting to swallow us up, and I cursed her for talking me into wearing a pair of wedges that were already killing my feet.

"Let's get a drink," she yelled over the music and pointed to the kitchen where another swarm of people waited.

I scanned the crowd as I followed behind her. Theo Hunt was the object of my search. He moved into the frat house during his freshman year—which is why I knew he'd be at the party. But I didn't see him anywhere.

"My feet hurt." I leaned back against the kitchen counter as Dillon started rummaging through the bottles of liquor.

"Stop being a pussy. Your legs look great." She didn't even

look up at me as she pulled a crystal clear bottle from the group of liquor bottles. "Ah ha."

She pushed an empty red Solo cup in my hand before unscrewing the lid off the bottle of vodka. "Should we make it a double?" She wagged her eyebrows at me as she began pouring the alcohol into my cup.

"It's our first college party. I say we can live a little." Plus, I had spent my entire summer interning for my dad. I was allowed to get a little wild. The wildest things got around Duncan Enterprises was leaving the office a couple hours early for a round of golf.

"Cheers." She tapped her cup against mine with a grin on her face, and it didn't drop as she brought the cup to her lips.

The liquor slid over my tongue, and I winced as my throat began to burn. Dillon didn't seem fazed. She drank it down like water, her face not showing an ounce of discomfort. But I wasn't surprised. Dillon didn't seem like she was scared of much—not that shot of liquor and definitely not all the guys who couldn't seem to take their eyes off her.

She appeared to be about as bothered by them as she was the liquor.

Loud cheering rang through the house from outside, and Dillon slipped her arm through mine without second thought before pulling me in that direction.

Two beer pong tables were set up on a large deck, and at least half the party was surrounding them as they watched the games play out.

"Ohhh." The crowd laughed and some cheered as one of the players missed his shot, but I couldn't see a thing. I stood on my tiptoes to try to get a better look. There was a sea of polo shirts - some pastels, some sharing school spirit - but they all looked the same. They looked the same as the guys from my hometown—the douchebags who thought they were hot shit because their parents had money. They treated me like I was one of them, I suppose in their eyes I was, but I was nothing like them. I refused to be. Theo wasn't like them either. No matter how much he tried to fit in, he always stood out. He was never one of them, but when my eyes finally found his handsome face, I prayed that he hadn't changed a bit.

His jaw was just as square as the last time I saw it, his hair the same shade of dirty blond, and I sighed a little when I was certain that his first year of football hadn't ruined his face in the least little bit.

I pointed over the crowd to where he stood at the end of one of the beer pong tables and nudged Dillon. "That's Theo."

Dillon pushed on my shoulders as she jumped in the air just a bit to get a better look.

"That's Theo?" she said as she laughed. "As in, 'my best friend Theo is a Kappa? I want to surprise Theo at this party tonight?' That fucking Theo?"

I didn't take my eyes off him as I answered her. "That would be the one."

It had been exactly three hundred and sixty days since Theo left our home town for college.

Three hundred and sixty days of text messages, at least a hundred days of FaceTiming, and three hundred and fifty-four days that I didn't get to touch him.

He only came home from school for six days.

Those six days felt like everything was exactly like it was before. I had my best friend back, the smell of his cologne wasn't a distant memory, and his hair still flopped over his forehead in a way that made my hand itch to brush it out of his handsome face.

But those six days came and went in the blink of an eye.

And then he was gone again.

But the plan we had been making for the past five years was

finally happening. One freshman, one sophomore, and one stupid pact. But the promise that we would go to the same college, that we would stay together no matter what, meant more to us than anything else.

When the University of Georgia offered Theo a full ride scholarship for football with the help of my dad, I tucked the letter I had received from Columbia University into the bottom of my panty drawer and tried not to think about it.

Theo expected me to follow him to the University of Georgia.

My parents expected me to follow in their footsteps at the University of Georgia.

And I couldn't swallow the thought of disappointing either.

Dillon smacked my arm trying to get my attention, and I winced as I looked down at her in shock. "The way you talked about him I thought he was going to be like a big cuddly teddy bear. You didn't tell me he was sex-on-a-stick Theo. Make your ovaries quiver Theo. Do whatever the hell you want with me Theo."

I actually chuckled because she wasn't wrong. "He's hot. Yeah?"

"How in the hell have you not fucked him?" Dillon leaned on some guy we didn't know this time to get a second look. "Like seriously? How long have you been friends?"

"Since we were twelve." I watched as he threw a ball and sank it in one of the cups. "He wasn't as hot back then." Actually, he was, but she didn't need to know that.

"And what? As he aged, your vagina shut down from his beauty?"

I rolled my eyes at her just as the party broke out in a loud cheer. I couldn't see a damn thing that was going on, but from the sound of things, the game was over, and people were clearly excited about the winner.

"Alright." The crowd quieted a bit as a guy tried to talk over them. "We have a new winner on table two. Theo and Cam." The crowd cheered again. "Do we have any new challengers?"

Hands shot up like crazy, but there was no way I wasn't getting in on this game. I clasped Dillon's hand in mine and jerked her forward as I squeezed through all the polo shirts.

"We want in," I called out as we finally pushed our way through the front of the crowd.

Theo's gaze slid over to me, and it took him a second to realize that I was standing in front of him. "Holy shit."

"Surprise." I held my hands out to the side like I had just performed the greatest trick and smiled at my best friend.

His matching smile was the best thing I'd seen since I arrived in this town.

He moved, and as soon as he was within touching distance of me, my feet left the ground. Theo spun me in his arms, and I took a deep breath for the first time in forever.

I buried my face in his neck and breathed in the smell of home. Not the home where my parents lived, but this home, with him.

"What are you doing here?"

My feet had no chance of touching the ground as he squeezed me against him.

"I came a couple days early." My words reverberated against his skin.

"You should have called me. I would have come to you."

He lowered me to the ground, my body pressing against his the entire time, and I blinked up at him. I could barely believe we were finally here.

"I'm here now." I tipped my head up, meeting his gaze.

"You are." He pulled me tighter against him and fingered a piece of my hair. "And just in time to get your ass whipped in beer pong."

"Keep dreaming, frat boy." I pushed against his chest, and his smile grew to the point that his dimples appeared. Those dimples were my favorite part of him.

"We've got our challengers, Sam," Theo called over his shoulder to the guy leading the games without taking his eyes off me.

Theo moved back to his side of the table, and I watched as more cups were placed on the table and beer was poured into each.

"Do you need me to remind you how to shoot? Line you up?" A slow smirk uncurled across his lips, and my heart quickened.

"I think I've got it."

From where I stood, I watched a group of girls stare at him like love-sick puppies as he took his first shot. I couldn't blame them, but all of their attention on him still made me uneasy. But I should have been used to it by now. He sank the shot, just as I knew he would, and I quickly popped the ball out of the cup with my finger before lifting the cup to my lips.

Theo's teammate, Cam, over-shot and the ball soared past us. He was cute in a way that most of the guys here were, but he looked just like them and nothing like Theo. A guy from the crowd tossed the ball back to Dillon, and she lined up before taking the first shot for our team.

The ball quickly bounced off the top of a cup before hitting Theo in the chest.

"You're already on the losing end, Maddy."

I stretched my arms out dramatically. "Don't worry. The champ is here."

"She's big talk," he said, loudly enough for everyone to hear.

Laughter broke out around us, and I smiled as I lined myself up directly across from where he stood at the other end of the table. Theo smiled at someone beside him as they said something I couldn't hear, and I took the opportunity to throw the ball directly at Theo's perfectly sculpted chest.

His mouth opened in shock as the ball bounced off his chest and landed dead center of the middle cup as if I had planned it that way.

"Ohhhh." All the friends who were laughing at his earlier joke went crazy, and I tried not to laugh but couldn't help it.

Theo didn't say a word. He just grinned as he lifted the cup to his mouth and chugged the beer.

The game continued on shot after shot until we were both down to only one cup. It was Theo's turn, and he hadn't missed a shot the whole game. He never missed a shot.

"I really feel bad for you, Maddy. You're going to lose in front of all of these people." He pushed up the sleeve of his white t-shirt and the curve of his bicep made me lose concentration for a minute.

"Show him your boobs to distract him." Dillon's words caught me off guard, and I snorted in laughter as Theo looked back and forth between us.

"Do not." Theo pointed his finger at me, but he knew I hated being told what to do.

I was always told what to do.

"Don't what?" I leaned forward a bit to where he could catch a glimpse of my cleavage at the top of my tank top. There was no way in hell I would pull out my breasts in front of all these people. Theo should have known that too, but I was just tipsy enough to make him think differently—to tease him just a little.

"Maddison Ray Duncan. I swear to God."

"What?" I shimmied the tiniest bit, and Cam laughed beside him before Theo smacked him directly in his stomach.

"You better take your shot, Hunt." I slowly slipped the

strap of my tank top off my shoulder, and Theo growled before quickly throwing his ball in our direction. It hit the rim of the single cup and slowly rolled along the edge in a circle as it made its way in. I didn't hesitate as I leaned forward and blew in the cup, causing the ball to bounce back out.

"No fucking way," Cam yelled just as I grabbed the ball off the table.

"Sorry for your luck, boys." Dillon and I high-fived each other like we had just won the game, but we still had one shot to make.

Theo was staring at me like he either wanted to kill me or kiss me, and I prayed it was the latter. I had been thinking about the latter for too many years to count.

"We have to win now," Dillon whispered where only I could hear.

"Then make your first shot of the night." I was talking to her, but I was still looking at him.

She flipped me off as she took a step back from the table and raised her arm in the air.

"Don't try so hard. Just look at the cup and let the ball slip through your fingers." I had been coaching her through most of the game, but her closest shot landed about a foot in front of the cups.

She still didn't listen to a single word I said this time either, and I watched in horror as she closed her eyes and tossed the ball forward without a semblance of aim. I held my breath as the ball soared through the air— one, two, three seconds. The ball hit the far edge of the cup almost knocking it over, almost causing us to lose the game, before it finally fell into the beer.

"Holy shit." I heard Theo's words just before the cheers broke out. I wrapped my arms around Dillon, and the two of us jumped up and down in celebration.

You would have thought we had just won an Olympic medal instead of a game intended to get you drunk.

"That game was rigged." Theo tugged on my hand and pulled me away from Dillon and toward him. Exactly where I wanted to be.

"Don't be a sore loser. It's not a good look on you." I flicked the thick piece of hair that hung over his forehead out of his face so I could see both of his brown eyes clearly.

"You don't think I look good?" He put his hand over his heart. "First, you kick my ass in front of practically the whole school. Then you call me ugly."

"A pretty boy like you." I let my fingers roam over his clean-shaven cheek just before I patted it mockingly. "No one could ever call you ugly."

He grinned and nipped at my fingers just as I jerked them away. "I can't believe you're finally here."

"Me either." I shook my head. "It doesn't feel real." I had been thinking about getting out of my parents' house for so long that I never thought it was going to happen. But I was finally here, and even though they still had just as much control over me, I still felt freer somehow.

"Stay with me tonight." He nodded toward the house that was still so filled with people I had no idea how anyone could sleep in it.

"I have Dillon with me." I wanted to stay with him. I wanted to stay more than I wanted anything else.

We used to stay the night together all the time growing up. He would sneak in my bedroom window when my parents were fighting or when his father was too drunk not to be cruel. We didn't stop when I had a boyfriend for a total of five days or when his girlfriends always seemed to have a problem with how much time he spent with me.

No one ever came between us. Not some girl, not some guy, and definitely not our parents.

Theo looked at my parents like they were gods, and I knew why. His father only cared about work, alcohol, and him doing well at football. They were the only things he had cared about since Theo's mother died when he was thirteen.

My parents were never so cruel. They loved me, but they didn't allow me to be anything other than exactly what they wanted. I knew it was pathetic to hate the way my parents controlled every single choice I made in my life, because I could have had it so much worse.

Theo had it so much worse.

But their control festered inside me with every new thing they demanded. Theo thought I was crazy. He saw two parents who loved me, who loved him, and I knew that's all I should have seen too.

"I'll make sure one of the DDs gets her home safe." He pulled me closer to him. "Just stay."

I had never been able to tell Theo no—not when he needed me and not when he was just jonesing for a bit of fun. I couldn't tell him no then, and I wasn't going to start telling him no now. "Okay."

CHAPTER 2

THEO LED me through the house and up the stairs. The hallway held so many doors that I wondered how many guys lived here. There had to be at least twenty.

Theo stopped at the third door on the left and pulled a key from his pocket.

"You lock your door?" I leaned up against the wall next to him as he slid the key in.

"Yeah. I don't want anyone fucking in my room during one of these parties."

"Good point." I laughed and tucked my hair behind my ear. My dorm room may have been tiny, but at least I didn't have to worry about that.

Theo flicked on the light in his room, and I followed him inside before closing the door behind us.

His room was clean except for the few pieces of clothes that littered the floor, and I smiled when I saw a picture of us together sitting on his dresser. It was the day after he graduated high school, we were at the lake with our friends, I was on his back about to jump in the water, and I had never been happier.

I had seen his room what felt like a million times before on the phone, but being here was different. I felt like I couldn't look around quick enough. I wanted to take in every single thing I saw. There were plenty of things that were familiar, but there was more that wasn't. It felt odd knowing that Theo had a life that I didn't know every detail of.

It felt wrong.

A t-shirt being tossed in my face brought my attention back to Theo.

"Your favorite."

I looked down at the ratty Sublime t-shirt that I had slept in so many times before and hugged it to my chest. "I don't know why you don't just give this to me."

"I still wear it." Theo chuckled softly as he dug through his drawer.

I rolled my eyes as I lifted the edge of my shirt and pulled it over my head. Theo's eyes tracked my movements, his eyes glued to my simple black bra. I had changed in front of him so many times before, but the way he watched me now was different. At least it felt different to me.

I slipped his t-shirt over my head as I watched him watch me, and I took a deep breath and tried not to seem affected. His cotton t-shirt was so worn that it felt like silk against my skin. I ran my fingers over the soft fabric, and I let the smell of him engulf me.

I popped the button on my shorts and pulled them down my legs before tossing my clothes onto his small desk that held nothing but football equipment. His shirt swallowed me whole and touched the tops of my thighs. He used to take it off his back for me sleep in it while he'd cuddle up next to me in nothing but a pair of shorts. I looked over at his tan abs and knew that nothing much had changed.

Theo sat down on the edge of his bed and hooked his finger in the small hole in his t-shirt near my belly button. "Come here." He pulled me toward him and wrapped his arms around my back as he rested his forehead against my stomach.

I pressed my fingers into his hair and let the strands slip through them. I could feel the stress leaving his body. Football had been kicking his ass with a summer filled with practices, workouts, and drills, but he never let up. He never took a break.

"Damn, I've missed you," he mumbled without lifting his head.

"You just missed my massaging skills." I chuckled and ran my fingers down the base of his neck.

He nodded his head. "One hundred percent."

"Hey." I slapped his shoulder playfully and his arms tightened around me.

My hands clung to his shoulders as he fell back onto the bed and pulled me along with him. I bounced against the mattress, my laughter uncontrollable as Theo dug his fingers into my sides.

"Stop." I barely managed to get the word out as I squirmed on the bed to get away from him.

"Did you miss me?" He tickled me harder.

"No!" I half yelled, half giggled.

"Maddison, you tell me that you missed me right now."

I lifted my foot and tried to kick him off me, but my effort was useless. He caught it in his hand before I could use it. His touch on the bare skin of my calf made my stomach tighten in a way that it shouldn't have been with my best friend.

"Not happening," I said, breathless, as I pushed against his chest, but he easily pinned my hands above my head.

His face was directly above mine, my breath was still rushing out in laughter, and he was smiling in a way I rarely saw him do unless we were alone.

In a way that I loved.

"Did you miss me?"

"Oh. Fine." I huffed. "I missed you."

He pushed my hair out of my face and pressed a small kiss to my forehead. "I know."

I rolled my eyes at his cocky grin and tried to calm my racing heart. "Did you miss me?"

His eyes were watching my lips as I spoke. "You know I did."

I wanted to kiss him. I wanted to kiss him more than I had ever wanted anything else, but I knew that the one simple move would have consequences.

That one simple touch would change everything.

But I still wanted it and part of me thought that he wanted it too. He was looking at me like he did.

But God, I wanted him to be the one to kiss me.

I pulled my bottom lip between my teeth. Theo watched, his gaze glued to the movement before he pushed off me and rolled onto his back beside me.

I couldn't stop the burning in my chest even though I tried not to let myself feel disappointed. He was being the smart one. I knew that, but it didn't do anything to make it easier.

We'd been walking this line between friendship and more for so long that I couldn't even remember a time when I was one hundred percent certain about what we were.

Best friends trying like hell not to be lovers.

The idea of not being with Theo in that way scared me, but the thought of losing him completely ripped me in two. And I had no doubt that the two of us would manage to fuck this up.

We'd fuck up everything.

But I still wanted it.

I wanted everything. I didn't want to be the girl who showed up to all his football games and watch him celebrate with someone else. I wanted to be his girl, his only girl, and I wanted every single one of his celebrations, his defeats. I wanted it all.

But I didn't know how to get off the sidelines. I felt forever stuck. I was his biggest cheerleader, but I didn't want to be stuck with pom-poms in my hands.

"I got you something." Theo stood from the bed, and the moment before was brushed away as easily as it came.

As easy as it had always been.

I grabbed a pillow and tucked it under my head as I watched him grab a grocery bag off the top of his dresser.

"You didn't." I laughed as he pulled out three boxes of chocolate covered raisins.

"Do you think I'd let my favorite girl come to college and not have her favorite thing in the world waiting on her?" He grinned before tossing a box in front of me.

I quickly opened the box and poured a few in my mouth. "God, I love you."

"I know." He fell back on the bed and laid his head against my stomach.

"I was talking to my candy. Not you."

He snorted before grabbing the box out of my hand and pouring some in his mouth. "Have you decided on a major yet?" He asked his question around his candy, and I rolled my eyes while thinking about what to tell him.

Did I decide on my major yet? Yes. Did my parents shoot it down faster than I could finish my complete sentence? Also, yes.

It wasn't that I was hiding the fact that I wanted to become a photojournalist from Theo, but I knew that he would be about as supportive as my parents.

And it was better that I just forgot it now.

There was no use wasting my dreams on something I could never have.

His football scholarship was here. My father's alma mater was here. I was meant to be here. Not in New York. Not at Columbia.

"I'm going to stay undecided for now. Keep my options open." I pulled the box of chocolate covered raisins from his hand and poured more in my mouth.

"You're the most indecisive person I know." He shook his head.

"Not true. I know for a fact that chocolate covered raisins are my favorite."

"What else?" He turned his head to the side and looked up at me.

"I know that black is my favorite color and summer is my favorite season."

"And I'm your favorite guy?" He arched one of his eyebrows at me.

"Always."

CHAPTER 3

MY BODY WAS ON FIRE.

Theo was pressed against my back, his skin a furnace against mine, and I felt like I could barely breathe as his weight pushed against me. There wasn't a single spot of my body that wasn't touched by him, but somehow I managed to wiggle inch by inch out from under him without waking him up.

It was still relatively dark outside, and I had to blink a few times to see clearly as I checked the time on my phone. Six forty-five in the morning.

I yawned and thought about climbing back into bed behind Theo, but my bladder was screaming at me and I knew I wouldn't make it a few more hours until he woke up.

I cracked open his door and looked up and down the dark hallway. The house looked different without a single person in sight. I tiptoed my way to the bathroom, and it was eerily quiet compared to the noise of the party last night.

There was a pair of boxers wadded up on the floor and I tiptoed over them so I could pee without someone's dirty clothes touching me. I wondered if those were taken off in haste. A little romp session on the bathroom counter or maybe against the bathroom door.

A lot more action than I got in the privacy of a bedroom.

I finished my business and looked at myself in the mirror. My hair was a bit wild from sleep, and Theo's t-shirt was wrinkled against my skin. It felt weird to be here. Not necessarily in this frat house, but here at college, where I wasn't suffocating under my parents' thumbs. Where I at least got to pretend that I had some freedom.

I barely knew what to do with myself without my parents dictating my every move.

The door to the bathroom stuck in a way that only seemed to happen in old houses, so I put two hands on the handle and pushed it open with all my strength. It opened with a loud groan and I ran directly into a wall or I guess a better description would be a wall of muscle.

I pushed against the guy's chest to keep my skin from touching his just as I noticed he was wearing nothing but a towel. A white, fluffy towel that barely covered a thing. His hand gripped my elbow trying to steady me, and I tried to calm my racing pulse from the embarrassment of his lack of clothing and mine.

"Oh, sorry." He fumbled for words and seemed as genuinely shocked as I was.

"It's okay." I tugged on the edge of Theo's t-shirt and tried not to look up at him. His stomach was on full display in front of me, and I let my eyes go there for only a moment before I jerked my gaze away and looked up at his face.

His dark hair was a wild mess and looked like he had been running his fingers through it for most of the night. Or someone else had. Either way, it had the same effect. His jaw was square and somehow made his beautiful face seem harsh, but his eyes were warm and a deep shade of blue that reminded me of something I couldn't quite put my finger on. I studied his face for an ounce of recognition, but I didn't see him at the party last night. I would have remembered him if I had.

His hand that was still pressed against my skin felt like it was burning me in the best possible way, and I knew I should have pulled away from him. But I didn't.

"I'm Easton." I watched his full lips as the sleep-filled, husky words slipped past.

"Maddison." My voice, on the other hand, sounded squeaky and anxious and far too affected by a guy I didn't know.

His gaze slowly slid down my body, and the threads of Theo's shirt felt like they were unraveling under his stare.

I desperately wanted to flee back to Theo's room. My heart

was racing, and I knew my cheeks were flushed with embarrassment. But for some reason, I didn't.

"You live here?" I asked like a complete and total idiot.

"Mmmmm..." He nodded but didn't take his eyes off of me. "You don't."

"No." I shook my head. "I'm here with Theo." The words came out, but I hated the way they sounded. I didn't know why, but I didn't want him to think I was here sleeping with Theo.

I didn't want him to think that I was that girl.

"Ahh." He ran his fingers through his hair and made a face as if he knew exactly what I was doing with Theo, and I hated it.

"He's my friend," I rushed out.

"Theo's got lots of those." He chuckled, and the sound pissed me off.

"No." I crossed my arms and his gaze slid to my thighs that were a bit more exposed. "I'm his best friend. From home."

"Alright, sweetheart." His tone was so condescending, so sure that he already knew everything that he needed to know about me.

"Alright, asshole." I started to push past him, but he smiled at me. A smile that could take your breath away if it wasn't attached to such a jerk.

His hand touched my elbow again, and I didn't know why I did it, but I stopped.

"I'm sorry. I shouldn't have said that. I was being an asshole."

I nodded in agreement. "You were."

"It's a little early for our first fight. Don't you think?" He grinned and I had a feeling that grin got him out of everything. Or into anything he wanted.

"Early in the day or in our relationship?" I cocked an eyebrow at him.

"Both." His hand moved to the edge of his towel to hold it in place, and I couldn't help following its descent. "How will we explain to our children that we became enemies before we figured out that we were actually in love?"

I actually laughed out loud at his attempt at a joke, and I took my time looking over every ridge of his toned stomach and chest before meeting his eyes again. "It would be heartbreaking. Especially, if they found out you were really never my type."

His smile was devastating as it lit up his face—devastatingly handsome, devastatingly treacherous.

"We can change that."

"You seem awfully sure of yourself for a man in nothing but a towel." I looked toward said towel again with a pointed stare.

"You don't like my towel? Do you want me to take it off?" His hand tugged on the edge as if he was going to drop it, and I squealed as I covered my eyes.

"No!"

His deep laugh surrounded me, and I peeked through my fingers to see him watching me with a smile.

"Are you decent?"

"I guess it depends on who you're asking, but I'd say I'm more than decent."

I pulled my fingers away from my face and pointed at him as I started backing away toward Theo's door. "You're too much."

"I've heard that a time or two as well." He winked at me, and it took everything inside of me to put my hand on Theo's door handle. I didn't want to leave him, but I knew how crazy that sounded. I just met the guy and his towel.

And Theo was just behind the door.

"Goodbye, Easton." I still couldn't stop smiling. I had never found it so easy to smile around someone. So easily pulled in.

"Bye, baby. Wait. Too soon? Maybe I'll wait until our next

meeting for the pet names." He was leaning against the door frame, and I had never met anyone so shameless.

"Until next time," I whispered as I slowly turned the handle.

"I can't wait." He kept his eyes on me as I disappeared through Theo's doorway.

The door creaked as I pushed it open, but Theo didn't move an inch as I closed it behind me and pressed my weight against it. I took a deep breath and tried to calm my racing heart as I stared at him sleeping.

I had been nervous around plenty of guys before. Too many had made my heart race over the years. Heck, Theo made my heart race daily, but this felt different somehow.

I pulled the blanket back and crawled into bed behind Theo one slow movement at a time. The warmth of him surrounded me as my body slid next to his, and as soon as he felt me, he turned in my direction and wrapped his arm around my middle.

I tried to let the comfort of him pull me to sleep as he pulled me tighter against his body, but every time I closed my eyes, all I could see were eyes of blue taunting me.

Wrapping my hand in Theo's, I let him engulf me - his smell, his warmth, everything that was uniquely him, and I tried to forget the guy from the bathroom who I'd probably never see again.

CHAPTER 4

"THIS IS the best pizza I have ever had." I crammed another bite of my pepperoni pizza in my mouth.

"I told you." Theo wiped some escaping sauce off the edge of my chin before taking another bite of his own food.

"I thought you were lying though. I've never had better pizza than The Pizza Brothers, but this." I held my pizza up for him to look at. "This is ridiculously good."

He grinned. "I wouldn't lie to you. Especially not about pizza."

"Uh huh," I mumbled around another bite.

"Are you ready for classes tomorrow?"

"I think so. I printed out all of my syllabuses and arranged my binders according to those."

Theo snorted. "You are such a dork."

"I am not." I put my hand over my heart. "It's called being prepared."

"It's called being a complete and total nerd."

I wadded up my napkin and threw it at his head, but he caught the pitiful attempt before it even had a chance to hit him.

"Nice try." He threw it down on the table before taking another bite of his pizza.

"Are you ready?" I arched an eyebrow at him. All Theo thought about was football. I would be surprised if he even knew what classes he was taking this semester.

"Not quite." He grinned at me. "I was hoping we could do a little school shopping today."

"The day before classes start?" I shrieked. "You're going to give me heart palpitations."

"That's what all the girls say."

I rolled my eyes dramatically, but something about his playfulness reminded me of Easton. I hadn't stopped thinking about him since our run-in this morning. "You are ridiculous. College has really gone to your head."

He smiled like he knew what I was saying was true but didn't care.

"Don't forget homecoming is in a couple weeks. You need to buy a dress for the Kappa formal." He took another huge bite of his pizza.

"Why is that even a thing?" I huffed even though I was glad that he asked me. Glad was an understatement. I couldn't believe that out of all the options I knew Theo had at his fingertips that he'd want to go with me. "I thought we ended formals in high school."

"Think again. I've had to get dressed up more times in one year of college than we did in all four years of high school."

"That makes me excited to start the school year," I said sarcastically.

"You look pretty in a dress." Theo threw out the compliment like it was nothing, but my stomach felt tight as the words slipped past his lips.

"But I feel comfortable in sweats." I saluted him with my pizza and listened to his deep chuckle.

"You're not wearing sweats to the formal. Your mom would die if she ever found out."

He wasn't wrong. She would take more offense to that than if I started doing drugs. "Fine. I'm going to get the puffiest dress I can find. Puffy sleeves and everything."

"That would be hot." He took another bite of pizza. "I'll have to fight all the boys away."

"You will." I nodded. "I doubt you'll even get a single dance in, I'll be looking so fine."

"Look who has a big head now."

I wiggled my eyebrows at him just as my phone started

vibrating against the table. "Speak of the devil." I watched the word Mom flash across my screen over and over.

"Are you not going to answer it?"

I shook my head and lifted my pizza to my mouth, but he was already grabbing my phone and hitting the speaker button.

"Hey, Mrs. Duncan. How are you?"

"Oh, Theo!" My mom sounded more excited to talk to him than she ever did with me. "How are you? Mr. Duncan and I have missed you so much."

She didn't even call my father by his first name. She never did when she was referring to him when talking to someone else. He was Mr. Duncan, the CEO of Duncan Enterprises, and the man who spent more time at the office than he ever did at home.

"I miss you all too." Theo smiled down at the phone even though my mom couldn't see him. "Maddy and I were just talking about you and what color you think she should wear to my homecoming formal."

I groaned and Theo covered the phone as he laughed at my discomfort. He knew that I hated talking to my mom about anything clothing related. She had strong opinions on my wardrobe, or lack thereof, and she could go on for hours about why I should choose a certain dress.

"Well, you know I love her in a soft pink." She gushed, and I practically gagged. "I could run into town and find her a dress. I'm sure I could find something lovely for her to wear."

"I've got it, Mom." I finally spoke for the first time as I flipped Theo off. "I think I've already found something."

"Oh." She sounded as affronted as I knew she probably was by the idea. "Well, remember which styles flatter your figure the most—"

"Yep," I cut her off before she could go any further. I was embarrassed for Theo to hear her speech about the size of my hips and the way fabric should drape over them. He had heard it all before. I just wasn't in the mood for it. I was never in the mood for it.

"Well, are you all set for your classes?" Her voice was tighter than it was just moments before, but I couldn't bring myself to care.

"Yeah. I have everything I need. Theo's not though. He hasn't even gone school shopping yet." I threw Theo under the bus, and he laughed because he knew I was trying to get the focus off me.

"He's so busy with football." She sounded so worried. "Theo, do you need me to go get some things for you?"

"That's alright, Mrs. Duncan. I'm going to force your daughter to go shopping with me in just a bit." He smirked in my direction.

"Good. Well, you two have fun."

"We will," Theo answered her just before the phone clicked off.

"You are such a suck up." He always had been. My mother adored him, and Theo made sure it stayed that way.

"Just because I'm your mama's favorite child doesn't mean you gotta hate me."

We both laughed, but he wasn't lying. I was pretty sure my parents would adopt him if they could. I was pretty sure that they fantasized about the two of us ending up together more than I did.

And that was saying something.

Because I thought about it a lot.

"Are you going to leave me hanging or are you going to help me?" Theo pouted his bottom lip out and batted his eyelashes in my direction. He didn't need to put in the effort. I would do anything for him.

"I'm all yours, slacker."

CHAPTER 5

MY FIRST CLASSES were going better than expected. I didn't fall asleep during Probability and Statistics, and I was at least fifty percent sure I would be able to take the class without completely bombing it, but that percentage was iffy.

Because I didn't math.

By the time English rolled around, I felt more confident in my surroundings and the subject, and I arrived ten minutes early to make sure I didn't miss a thing.

I watched as student after student made their way into the room. Some of them were early like me, and some of them were sprinting in the door and looked like they had just run across campus. One of the latter took the seat right next to me, and I tried not to laugh when she asked me if I had an extra pencil.

"I'm Imani by the way." She took the pencil I was holding out to her. I had at least ten more in my backpack.

"Maddison."

"You're a life saver." She saluted me with the pencil before pulling a notebook of her own out of her purse. I tried not to stare at the doodles that covered page after page as she tried to find a blank one, but they were incredible.

She didn't even look up as the professor started talking. She just started scratching my pencil into the page in a random pattern that made no sense to me.

Professor Bryant was an older man, and I watched the way random pieces of his hair stuck out to the side as he introduced himself. He had been with the University of Georgia going on twenty years, he was passionate about English and literature, and even though he seemed a bit crazy, I was oddly fascinated by him.

"I would love to know your name and your favorite book, if you even read," he grumbled just as there was a commotion at the door. "Ah, it's nice of you to join us."

The entire class looked toward the door ready to see an

embarrassed student who was late for the first day of class, but it was his dark brown hair that made me sit up straighter in my seat. It looked different than it did when I ran into him in the bathroom. No longer disheveled, it was perfectly pushed back out of his face and made him look more mature. Older than I would have originally guessed.

"Ladies and gentlemen, I would like for you to meet my teaching assistant for the semester, Easton Cole."

Easton moved around Professor Bryant's desk, and I heard a small groan from one of the girls behind me, followed by muffled laughter.

My stomach tightened as he set his bag down next to one of the chairs and faced us. He was attractive in a way that it almost felt wrong to call him handsome. It was something else. Something wildly alluring. Something that felt tempting in a way that you knew shouldn't.

"It's nice to meet you all." Easton's voice was as rough as it was the morning I met him, and I swear half the girls in the class weren't even breathing.

It was impossible not to be captivated by him, to not notice him, but he didn't notice me. Hell, he probably hadn't given me a second thought, but I had thought about him.

He pulled off his leather jacket before taking a seat behind the desk as Professor Bryant pointed to the first student and the introductions began. Each person said their name and the name of a book they probably had never read, but I was barely listening. Instead, I was sneaking glances at Easton as he pulled things out of his bag.

A smack to my arm pulled my attention away from him, and I looked over at Imani just as her hand left my skin.

"What?" I whispered.

She pointed a finger toward the professor, and I looked up just as a few laughs rang out around me.

"Oh." I sat up straighter in my chair, embarrassed to be caught ogling the TA. "I'm Maddison Duncan and my favorite book is... that's a hard question actually. My first instinct is to say the Harry Potter series, but I also love The Great Gatsby, Pride and Prejudice, Emma, I could keep going."

Professor Bryant smiled. "All excellent choices."

"Thanks." I tucked my hair behind my ear as he moved on to the next student.

I glanced up in Easton's direction, hoping to catch another glimpse of him, but this time he was staring straight at me. I shifted in my seat and looked away before allowing myself to look at him again. His gaze didn't shift an inch.

He seemed to be studying me. My breathing slowed as I watched the way he was looking at me. I felt exposed by the one simple look, like he was seeing more of me than I was willing to show.

His brow crinkled as he looked down at his desk, and I would have given anything to know what he was thinking. But when he looked back up, there was a sudden aloofness that hadn't been there only a moment before, and he didn't look in my direction again.

I knew because I couldn't take my eyes off him.

The professor continued around the class before he handed out our syllabus. The list of assignments and projects for this class seemed overwhelming compared to the simple syllabus that was posted online. He went over paper after paper that were listed with due dates, and I knew that I would have a long evening of writing everything into my planner.

Professor Bryant started shaking a baseball cap in his hands. "Let's start this semester off right and pick your partner for your group project."

Deep groans of frustration echoed around the room, causing Professor Bryant to roll his eyes.

"You're college freshmen. Just think, your partner could be your first friend while you're here or maybe even your enemy if you get a lazy partner."

A couple people laughed, probably the lazy ones, as more groans rang out. The professor ignored the groans and walked to the back of the room. He held out the ball cap to each student as he walked by and had them draw a piece of paper.

"Each of you will be paired up with another student in this class and you will have five weeks to complete the project. You each have an approved list of literature that you can choose from, and as the project is outlined on page three of your syllabus, you will each read the literature, compare your views of the work, and find a point that the two of you disagree on." Professor Bryant snapped his fingers. "That's where the magic happens. I want the two of you to argue about why you feel the way you do while trying to convince your partner to see your viewpoint. Then you will present your points to the class."

He held the hat out to me, and I said a quick prayer that I got a partner who would do their part of the work. I had enough on my plate already. I didn't need the added pressure of carrying one of my classmates.

My fingers connected with one of the last papers left, and I pulled it out before he continued on.

"I got ten. What did you get?" Imani was leaning over her desk toward me.

I carefully unfolded the white slip of paper to see it was blank. I flipped it over in my hands and the opposite side was empty as well.

"Alright. Get up. Get up." Professor Bryant waved us out of our desks. "Go find your partner."

I stayed in my spot and looked over my slip of paper again. When no number magically appeared, I raised my hand.

"Can't find your partner?" He put his hands against my desk.

"My paper is blank." I turned it over in my hands for him to see.

"Ah. Yes." He looked toward his desk. "Follow me."

I hesitantly climbed out of my chair and took a step down toward his desk. I tried not to look at Easton as we came closer and closer to him, but it was impossible.

"This class has an odd number of students, so you will be partnering up with Mr. Cole."

My feet skidded against the tile floor and I stopped in my tracks. "What?"

"He'll do his part. I promise you that." Professor Bryant smiled like he had just told the funniest joke just as Easton looked up at me.

I didn't dare look away from my professor.

"That's not necessary. I can do the project on my own."

"You're going to have an opposing view and argue with yourself?" He arched an eyebrow at me like I was insane.

"I can come up with an opposing view and figure out what that viewpoint might argue to make me see things their way."

Professor Bryant looked in Easton's direction then back at me. I could feel Easton watching me— his gaze burning into me. "I know you pulled the short straw here." The professor chuckled. "But Mr. Cole won't bite. He's actually got pretty strong opinions about each piece of literature on the list. I'd say that gives you a leg up."

He started heading back toward the other students. "I'll let you two get to know each other."

I shifted on my feet and slid my hands into my back pockets. "So." I finally slid my gaze to Easton. "Do you have a preference for which book we choose?"

He rubbed his hand over his jaw as the corners of his mouth jerked up. "It's your project, Maddison. You choose."

"The Awakening," I said the first book that came to mind from the list.

"Good choice."

"So, can you meet at the library on Friday to get started or do you need more time to read?"

"I'll be prepared. Don't worry about me." He tapped the edge of his red pen against the desk.

I looked around the room and everyone seemed to still be talking about their project.

"Okay. What times works for you on Friday?"

"I can be there by four. Does that work for you or will you need to be getting ready for the party?"

"What party?" I crossed my arms.

"There's a party at our house every weekend." His gaze ran over my neck as I toyed with my necklace. "I assumed you'd be there."

"Don't make assumptions about me."

His small smile turned into a full-fledged grin at my attitude, and I didn't even know why I had one. Easton made me feel nervous. He felt unpredictable and risky, and I hated that I had spent so much time thinking about him since I first met him.

"I just thought since you and Theo are best friends," he said it like it was a question. "You'd be there with him."

"I don't even know if Theo is going."

"Theo's going. Trust me. He never misses a party."

The fact that he felt like he knew something more about Theo than I did or the fact that he actually did made me even more irritated.

"What about you? Isn't it your frat too?"

"It is." He nodded his head. "I'm not much for parties these days."

"Why not?" I didn't know why, but I was intrigued by him. Even though he was the last person in this entire room who I wanted as my group project partner, I wanted to know more about him. But my interest in Easton was less than professional. I knew plenty of guys like Easton Cole, and I had no business having any interest in him whatsoever.

"Alright." Professor Bryant's voice called through the room. "That's it for today. I hope you and your partner scheduled some study dates."

I looked at Easton as he looked back down at the paper in front of him with a smile on his face. "I'll see you Friday, partner."

CHAPTER 6

THE REST of my week seemed to drag by. I had two other classes throughout the week, and they both went by without an ounce of excitement.

When I got to English again on Wednesday, I couldn't concentrate as I watched the door for any trace of Easton, but he never showed.

But I shouldn't have cared.

Easton was funny and handsome, and even though I couldn't stop thinking about him, he was also my TA, Theo's frat brother, and completely off limits.

Dillon was sitting at the table we had claimed all week in the campus cafeteria when I walked in with my tray of food on Friday.

"Do you have a date?" She ran her narrowed eyes over every inch of me.

"What are you talking about?" I pulled out the seat across from her and pulled the plastic lid off my salad.

"You look different today. What did you do?"

"I didn't do anything. You're crazy." I tried to avoid looking at her as I covered my healthy salad in a tub of ranch dressing.

"No. I'm not." She was still staring at me. "You're wearing more makeup than normal. Wait. Did you curl your hair?"

"I didn't have classes this morning." I brushed her off and hoped she bought it. "I didn't have to rush to get ready."

"Uh huh." She huffed skeptically before snapping her fingers. "Don't you have that group project today?"

I stuffed a huge bite of salad into my mouth and nodded my head like it was no big deal. Like I hadn't been freaking out all week about being alone with Easton. Who cares that we'd be in the library where there will probably be a hundred other students.

All I could think about was me and him.

"Who did you say your partner is?"

"I didn't." I unscrewed the cap of my water and took a long sip.

"Okay. Well, it's time to spill the beans."

"It's not a big deal."

"Obviously." She waved her hand in my direction, and I cursed myself for spending so much time on my hair and makeup. I knew I was overdoing it.

"I got partnered up with the TA."

"What?" She practically choked on her candy bar as she laughed.

"Male or female TA?"

I rolled my eyes. "Male."

"Ohh. An older guy. I totally approve."

"How do you approve if you don't even know who he is? He could be forty years old and going to college for the first time. Or he could be a total slob."

"Is he a slob?"

"No." I shook my head.

"Is he hot?"

I took another bite of my salad and nodded my head again.

She let out a small squeal, and I reached across the table to cover her mouth before the entire student body looked our way.

"What's his name?" Her lips moved against my hands.

"I'm not telling you."

"What?" She jerked my hands away from her mouth. "You have to tell me."

"No. I don't. You have a loud mouth and a wild imagination."

"Does Theo know about your study date with the handsome older guy?" She wiggled her eyebrows at me.

"First of all, you're insane. Second, why would I tell Theo?"

"Because it might make him jealous." She looked at me like I was an idiot. "Hello, friend zone. I'd like to get out of you."

I rolled my eyes even though she hit the nail on the head and looked down at the time on my phone. "Theo doesn't care about my group project, trust me. What about you? You have any big plans tonight?"

"Well." She leaned closer to me so no one could overhear our conversation. "As a matter of fact, I have a date with Cam."

"Theo's friend, Cam?" I had met him briefly at the party, but I didn't know anything about him other than he was also a part of Theo's fraternity.

"That's the one." She sighed like she already had it bad. "I saw him on campus this morning, and he asked if I'd like to go to dinner before going to their party after."

"What if the date is horrible? Then you're going to be stuck at a party with him." I made a horrified face, making her laugh.

"If it's that bad, I'll nine one one text you, and you'll come save me from my misery."

"Oh." I clapped my hands together like she was promising me the moon. "I've never had to do one of those before. I need to start thinking of my life crisis now."

She cocked her head to the side and assessed me with far too much seriousness. "Did you have no girlfriends growing up?"

"I did, but I wasn't super close with any of them. Not close enough to have like explosive diarrhea to help them get out of a bad date."

Dillon patted my hand and looked at me in pity. "You really are going to have to start thinking about your excuse now. Diarrhea isn't going to help me. I need your cockatoo to die or something."

"Faking the death of my cockatoo is bad juju."

"You don't have a cockatoo, so it doesn't matter. Hopefully my date will be magical, and you won't even hear from me." She sighed like she was a Disney princess about to be rescued when she was in a situation she could clearly handle on her own.

"I'll keep my phone on just in case."

...

I pulled my notebook out of my bag and laid it on the table near the back of the library. I couldn't believe how damn quiet the library seemed with so many people in it. I looked over the questions I had written down for Easton and me to discuss about the book and tried to think if there was anything else we would need to cover.

I wanted to be as prepared as possible. Not only did I not want to look like an idiot, but I also wanted to make this the least amount of awkward as possible.

And the chances of me being awkward as hell were pretty high.

The chair across from me drug against the ground, and I looked up just in time to see Easton smiling at me as he took a seat. A few people were looking over at us from the loud noise, but he didn't seem to notice.

"Hello, Maddison."

"Hello..." I hesitated. "What should I call you? Easton or Mr. Cole?"

His deep chuckle wasn't built for the library. "For the love of God, do not call me Mr. Cole. Only the professor does that."

I shifted a little in my seat. "Okay. Well, hello, Easton. Did you read the book?"

"About four years ago." He was still smiling at me.

"Do you need to reread it? Refresh your memory." You know. So I wouldn't fail this project.

"Nah." He tapped against his temple. "I have a great memory."

I rolled my eyes and picked up my pen. "Okay. I've come up with some discussion questions."

He completely ignored what I was saying. "What's your major?"

"Undecided." I tapped my pen against my paper.

"The girl who prepares discussion questions for the first day of our group project is undecided?" He shook his head.

"I'm sorry to disappoint you." I hated that he seemed to already see through me.

"The only thing disappointing me is this new roadblock in our future. Our poor children."

I rolled my eyes and watched him as he watched me.

"Well, Ms. Undecided. What do you want to do?"

"I just told you."

He waved me off. "I'm not asking what's your major. I'm asking what you want to do."

"Isn't that the exact same question?"

"Not always." He was resting in his chair like we weren't just having a casual conversation about the rest of my life.

"I don't know." At least that was what I kept telling myself over and over. It made it easier to swallow.

"Really? There's nothing that you love. Nothing you would choose to do if money, success, and all that shit didn't matter."

"You're nosey. Has anyone ever told you that?"

"They have." He leaned forward in his chair, a few inches closer to me. "Just answer my question, and I'll answer one of yours."

"Who says I want to know anything about you?" I did. God, I totally wanted to know everything about him, but I wasn't about to let him know that.

"Ouch, freshman. You wound me." He rubbed his hand over his chest.

"How old are you?" The question slipped past my lips without much thought.

"Old enough to be your TA." He arched one of his dark eyebrows.

"Which is?" I didn't want an answer that I already knew. I wanted the truth.

"Twenty-one."

He was a bit older than I expected, but I should have known. He had to at least be a junior or a senior to be a TA.

"Your turn." He nodded in my direction.

"I'm eighteen."

The corner of his mouth jerked into a small smile. "I figured that. I'm talking about what you love."

"Oh." I could feel heat rising in my cheeks. "Photo-journalism."

"Really?" He sounded like he was actually interested. "That's cool. They have a pretty good journalism program here."

"Yeah." I nodded my head because I already knew that. I knew that even though I wouldn't be majoring in journalism at the University of Georgia. My parents had it all planned out for me. If I wanted them to support me through college, I would be majoring in business. Then I was expected to work for my father.

"But you aren't going to pursue it?" He asked the question like he already knew the answer.

"What's your major?" I was tired of talking about me.

He tapped his finger against the book in front of me. "English."

"Oh. Of course." I felt like an idiot. "What are you planning to do with your English degree?"

"Well, I want to get my master's degree. I want to be a professor."

That would be a distracting English class.

"So, what you're telling me is that I should get a one hundred on this project since my partner is a professor in training."

"I'd say we have a pretty good shot. I'll even take your picture when you get the blue ribbon."

I rolled my eyes at him but couldn't stop smiling.

"I might need to borrow your camera though."

I lifted my phone and shook it. "It takes pretty good ones."

"A photojournalist without a camera. That's tragic."

"I'm not a photojournalist." I straightened myself in my seat and tried not to fidget.

"Oh right." He cupped his hand around his mouth as if he was sharing a secret with me. "A closet photojournalist."

"Are we going to work on the project or not?"

He laughed, and the sound seemed to run over every inch of me.

"Let me see your questions." He held his hand out toward me, and I hesitantly handed him my notebook. "These are good. You sure you don't want to be an English major?"

"I'm positive." I laughed.

"Okay. Let's do this."

His bottom lip was slightly fuller than his top lip, and I watched the way they moved as he read the question out loud. I swear I barely heard a thing he was saying. He was discussing his thoughts on my question, and all I could think about was what those lips would feel like against mine.

"What do you think?" His tongue peeked out of his mouth and wet his bottom lip.

"What?"

"The first question." He tapped his finger against my notebook. "What are your thoughts?"

"Oh. Right? The Awakening. My thoughts." I tucked my

hair behind my ear and started rambling about everything I had prepared to say the night before.

Easton was smiling at me again, and I swear that my gaze traveled to his mouth with every couple of words I spoke.

"Those are excellent points."

His words surprised me because our opinions were polar opposites. "Did I sway you to my side?"

"I'd say you're pretty convincing." He grinned.

My phone dinged beside me and I looked down to see a message from Theo.

Theo: What are you doing tonight?

"Are you hungry?"

I looked up from my phone. "What?"

"Hungry. Food. Dinner."

"We've only finished one question." I looked down at my notebook.

"And we have plenty of time to do the others. We can even discuss them over food. I'm not a good partner when I get hangry."

I couldn't stop smiling. "Do I get to pick where we eat?" I arched an eyebrow at him.

"That depends on what you pick."

"Chinese food." I rubbed my stomach over my shirt. "Do ya'll have any good Chinese food in this town?"

Easton closed my notebook and stood. "Grab your bag. I'm about to blow your socks off."

My stomach tightened in excitement as I did what he said. "I have pretty high standards," I joked.

"Noted." The way he smiled at me made me think that we were talking about more than food.

I followed him as he led us out of the library, but stopped when he turned right. "My car's over there." I pointed in the opposite direction.

"We're walking." He tugged on the strap of my bag until it fell in his hand. "It's only about a block from campus."

He started walking again, and I had to jog a few steps to catch up with him after my hesitation.

"Okay. I can carry my own bag though."

"I heard your thoughts on men in classic literature, freshman. I don't need anyone talking shit about me like that."

I rolled my eyes but didn't push the subject more because who was I to refuse a gentleman. A gentleman who I wasn't expecting to be so attracted to. Sure, his high cheekbones only seemed to accentuate his pouty lips and his dark hair was kind of wild in the wind.

But I had been able to resist both of those things before.

We turned a corner and kept walking past the college buildings, and Easton reached his hand out to me as he jumped down from the sidewalk to cross the street. My hand was only in his for a brief second, but as my fingers slipped from his, I already craved his touch.

Other than the small glance he gave me over his shoulder, I wasn't sure he even noticed that he had done it at all.

Easton held the door open for me, and I slipped under his arm to head inside.

"Easton!" an older lady behind the counter shouted his name before quickly moving in our direction.

He didn't hesitate as he opened his arms and gathered her in a tight hug.

"I've missed you." She patted him on the shoulder as they finally let each other go.

"I've missed you too. But my figure hasn't been missing your cooking." He patted his stomach and I couldn't stop thinking about what laid under his black t-shirt.

She smacked his arm and pushed him to the side to look at me. "Who is this?"

"Mei, this is Maddison. Maddison, this is Mei."

"It's nice to meet you," I said, smiling.

"You too. Come, come." Mei waved us to follow her toward the back of the restaurant, and I slid into the booth across from Easton.

Mei set a couple menus in front of us before heading back to the front to help another customer.

"You come here often?" I asked as I looked over the menu.

"You can say that." He chuckled. "I worked here my freshman and sophomore year."

"No way. So you have all the insider secrets?" I tapped my fingers together as he chuckled. "So, what would you recommend?"

"Everything here is good." His eyes roamed over the menu. "But the General Tsao's chicken is fucking amazing."

"I don't know if I trust you."

"You should." He looked up at me, and I swear the deep blue of his eyes turned molten.

"Do you have any references?" I propped my hand on my chin and stared at him.

"References?" He scratched at his jawline. "Job references? Mei will vouch for me." He nodded his head toward the front of the store. "Character references? I could call my mom."

He smiled, and I couldn't help joining him.

"No exes that will vouch for you?" I didn't know why I asked him that. Easton Cole was off limits to me. Not only could he get in trouble for being involved with a student, but he was also older than me. Not to mention he was Theo's frat brother.

"Oh." He shook his head in laughter. "Do we really want to go there?"

"Why not? I might find out about your sordid past?"

He leaned forward, just a couple inches closer to me, and

lowered his voice. "Exactly. I'm an authoritative figure to you now. I can't have you knowing all about my deep dark secrets."

"So, we went from future husband to authoritative figure just like that, huh?" I snapped my fingers.

There was no hesitation in his smile, and I loved that. He was so easy to be around. So easy to feel comfortable with.

"I blame you for that. You just had to take the one English class where I was TAing, huh?"

"I blame fate." I shrugged my shoulders.

"Fate?" His forehead scrunched in confusion.

"Yeah. Maybe it was fate that we met in your bathroom then fate again that you were my TA. Maybe the universe was showing us that we're going to be the best of friends."

I couldn't help but grin as I spoke because with every word that passed my lips, his forehead creased deeper.

"Thrown straight into the friend zone. Damn." He grinned as he pushed his hair out of his face.

"It's not such a bad place to be. I'm a pretty awesome friend."

He arched an eyebrow at me. "Has anyone actually ever told you that or is this a self-proclaimed affirmation?"

I opened my mouth in shock and pressed my hand to my chest. "You don't think I'm fun? I'm so fun."

"I didn't say that." He shook his head quickly. "I'm just saying maybe you're not as fun as you think you are."

"You can ask Theo. I'm the best."

The laughter in his eyes fell the smallest bit, and I wished I had never even said Theo's name.

"What's the deal with you two anyway?"

"Me and Theo?" I tucked my hair behind my ear. "We grew up next door to each other. We've been best friends for as long as I can remember."

"So, he's in the friend zone too?" He laughed, but it sounded a bit forced.

"He kind of rules my friend zone actually."

"So I have some competition."

"You could say that." I didn't know what it was about him, but bantering with him was the most fun I had in a while. I knew how pathetic that sounded. I was a college freshman for crying out loud. Not some spinster who hadn't seen a strapping young man in too many years to count.

But I was enamored by him just the same.

Mei came back to our table carrying two waters and both of us place our orders. I followed his suggestion and ordered the General Tsao's chicken, the same as him. He smiled as I did, and I had never been so intrigued by someone's smile before. Especially from someone who seemed to give it away so freely.

There was a quiet lull between us. The silence of getting to know each other, but for some reason, it didn't feel awkward like it should have.

"Should we play twenty-one questions?" I laughed at my stupid question, but his eyes lit up.

"Only if I get to go first."

"Shoot." I sat up farther in my seat and prepared myself for his questions.

"What's your favorite movie?" He was watching me so intently, and it was weird. I didn't think I had ever been so noticed before, so truly noticed.

"Starting with the hard questions first." I took a sip of my water. "Harry Potter."

"Which one?" He narrowed his eyes like one wrong answer from my lips could ruin everything.

"All of them. I refuse to pick a favorite, so don't make me."

"Okay then. What's your first question?" He stretched his arm out, resting it on the back of the booth causing his t-shirt to stretch across his chest. I couldn't stop staring as I thought of a question to ask him.

"Why are you in a fraternity?"

Theo had joined for the parties that came with being a frat member and because half the football team were also members, but Easton didn't seem like the type.

"I got a scholarship when I joined." He had no shame in sharing his answer. "It pays for a quarter of my tuition."

I wanted to nod in understanding, but honestly, I couldn't. My parents had paid for my education like the cost was nothing to them, and in reality, I guess it wasn't. I knew I was blessed, but there was something about knowing that Easton had to work for what he wanted, that he had to join a fraternity he didn't seem to fit into just to get an education. It made me feel guilty.

"Do you have any tattoos?" He wiggled his eyebrows, and I laughed at his preposterous question.

"Absolutely not. My mother would have a coronary."

"Your mom strict?" he asked, but I didn't answer him.

Instead, I shook my head. "Don't get greedy. It's my turn."

He chuckled, and I thought about my next question.

"Do you have a girlfriend?"

He grinned, a dazzling grin that made my stomach tighten, and shook his head. "Not at the moment. What about you?"

I should have laughed at his question. It was a joke really, because I hadn't had a decent prospect for dating since I broke up with Josh Lowe after I lost my virginity to him when I was sixteen years old.

"No."

Mei returned to our table with our food, and I was thankful. I didn't want to start rambling about my love life or lack thereof.

I stabbed my fork into a bite of chicken and moaned as the flavor hit my mouth.

"I told you," Easton boasted. "It's the best ever."

"Are you from Georgia originally?" It was starting to feel more like two people just genuinely getting to know each other versus a game of twenty-one questions.

"I am. Northern Georgia, but it still counts." He took a bite of his food, and I could see him thinking of his next question as he ate. "Tell me one thing that's on your bucket list."

"My bucket list?" I scrunched my nose. "Do people seriously have those?"

"They do." He nodded like I was crazy. "Come on. Tell me one thing you've always wanted to do."

"I don't know." I laughed as a series of things that would piss my parents off ran through my head but none of those were real. "It's stupid, really."

"It's not stupid. Just tell me."

"I've always wanted to go to a drive-in movie. You know the kind where you stay in your car and listen to your movie on the radio."

He was grinning at me.

"You know? Like in *Grease*?"

"I know what a drive-in movie is." He chuckled as he ran his fingers through his hair.

"Then why are you looking at me like that?"

There were a million things I expected him to say. *Because your bucket list item is dumb, because other people want to cure cancer, because a drive-in movie is as lame as you are.* But the last thing I expected to come out of his mouth was, "Because you're so damn cute."

CHAPTER 7

I HESITATED at the front door. I didn't really know the rules of a frat house. Was I supposed to knock? Should I just walk in?

Every time I had been here before, I had been with Theo. It felt weird actually. To not be here with him. It felt like I was doing something wrong even though I wasn't.

I pulled my phone out of my pocket and sent Easton a quick text.

Easton: Be right there.

His gray sweatpants hung low on his hips, and they were the first thing I noticed as he opened the door.

"I almost thought you were going to bail."

I looked up at him, slowly, taking in all the details that assured me that coming here was, in fact, a bad idea.

"I'm five minutes early."

He put his hand on the door frame, and I was far too interested in the way the muscles of his arm shifted with the movement.

"Yeah, but you seem like the type that shows up at least twenty minutes early." He smiled at me, and he was right. I had been sitting in my car for the last ten minutes at least, but I wasn't telling him that.

I pushed against his stomach, forcing him to move out of my way. "I'm not that predictable, am I?"

He was staring down at me, and even though I knew I should have moved my hand away from him, I let his warmth seep into my fingertips as I stepped farther into the house.

"No." He barely shook his head. "I guess you're not."

Easton pushed the door closed behind us, and I let my hand fall away from him as the latch rang out around us.

"Do you want anything to eat or drink before we head upstairs?" Easton didn't step away from me, and I realized that I hadn't been this close to him since the first day I met him. I hadn't allowed myself this close.

Because everything about him was more potent when I couldn't seem to escape it.

"No. I'm fine."

"Okay." He hesitated, only a second longer, before he moved away from me and headed up the stairs. The same stairs that I had taken with Theo so many times before.

We stopped three doors down from Theo's. I didn't know why I stared at his door when we passed. I knew he wouldn't be here today. Not that it mattered. Theo was my best friend and Easton was my partner in a group project. I just needed to repeat that over and over in my head.

Neither of these guys were for me.

I took in Easton's room as I stepped inside. The walls were a crisp white, but one of them was covered from floor to ceiling in bookshelves that was crammed with books in every nook and cranny. A large bed was in the middle of the room and the dark grey comforter was thrown haphazardly over it. His desk was made of dark wood and took up a large majority of the space.

The scent of him, the spicy hint of cologne, the clean fragrance of detergent, I took a moment to breathe it in because I couldn't help it.

Easton sat down on his bed, his back against his headboard, his legs laid out in front of him, and for a moment, I felt weak in the knees over how handsome he was.

"Would Professor Bryant approve of us working on this project in your room?"

He ran his hand through his hair and looked up at me with indecision warring in his eyes. "No. I guess he wouldn't."

A small thrill shot through me.

I set my backpack at the foot of his bed before pulling out my notebook and pen. He was watching me, but I let my eyes roam around his room to attempt to calm my racing heart.

I moved toward his desk, but the sound of his hand patting the bed stopped me.

"You can sit on the bed. I promise I won't bite."

I smiled and tried to hide my nervousness behind the fake gesture. I didn't like him knowing that he was affecting me even though he wasn't even trying.

"We only have a couple more questions left." I climbed on the foot of the bed where I could face him, but we weren't at risk for touching. "Then I'll type everything up and we can go over it."

"So, you'll only be forced to be around me a couple more times." He pouted, pushing his bottom lip out dramatically.

I wanted so badly to lean forward and pull that lip between my teeth.

"Like you need to force girls to hang out with you." I rolled my eyes and opened my notebook. "I'm surprised you didn't already have plans for today."

"I can juggle." He winked at me and I threw my pen at his chest.

"Ha ha."

His smile was devastatingly beautiful as he rubbed his chest where the pen hit. "Don't worry, you're my only group project. You have my undivided attention."

I tried not to stare as the bottom edge of his t-shirt lifted and fell with the movement.

"I'm not sure if that should make me feel better or worse." I looked around me. "Are these sheets clean? Maybe I should sit at the desk."

I made my way to climb of the bed, but Easton grabbed my foot before I could move an inch. "Don't even think about it." He pulled me toward him just a fraction. "The sheets are clean. I promise."

My skin tingled where his hand was still pressing against

my foot, and I thought about how many times I had been in a similar situation with Theo. How many times I had wanted him to kiss me. It had never felt like this.

"Where should we start?" His thumb ran over my ankle and I felt that simple touch all the way to my core.

"I'm sorry?" I was staring at his hand and silently begging it to move again.

"The questions." His hand moved then, and he tapped his fingers against my notebook. "Where do you want to start?"

"Oh." I quickly looked at my notebook and prayed he didn't notice the blush that I could feel heating up my cheeks. "Um. Let me look."

I scanned over the questions, and I tried to figure out where we last stopped. When I finally found my place, I read the question out loud before finally looking up at him.

"You're really cute when you get flustered." He was so relaxed, so at ease, and I felt like my heart was trying to break out of my chest.

"I'm not flustered," I lied. We both knew I was.

But he let me get away with it.

"Have you ever been wakeboarding?"

My head spun with the different directions he was taking the conversation.

"What?"

"You." He pointed his finger toward me. "Wakeboard. Behind a boat."

"Absolutely not."

"Do you want to?" There was a bit of mischief in his eyes as he asked the question, and even though I ached to reach out and touch it, I had more sense than that.

"Absolutely not." I chuckled as I shook my head as I looked back to my notebook.

"Come on." He leaned forward and covered the notebook

with his hands. "A few of my friends are going tomorrow. You should come. You can hang out on the boat if you don't want to try, but it will be fun."

I stared down at his hands and tried to come up with a reason as to why I shouldn't go. Sure, I had school work to do, but I was already a little ahead in most of my classes.

"If we get this project done today, I'll think about it." It was a half answer, but it was the only one I was willing to give him at the moment.

"Deal."

He scooted closer to me and started discussing the question for our project. I quickly picked up my pen and wrote down key pieces of his argument, and I somehow managed to do it without giving the words he was saying any thought.

Instead, I was thinking about how close his body was to mine, and how easily he asked me to hang out with him tomorrow. There was no pretense of the group project, no reason, other than to spend time together. I thought about what his friends were like. Would they all be upperclassmen? Would they know that Easton was actually my TA?

"What about you?" He ran his hand through his hair, and I watched as each strand fell back into place.

"Sounds good."

My gaze snapped back to him at the sound of his deep chuckle. "You're supposed to be arguing, freshman."

"Right." I straightened my spine and tapped my pen against the paper. "But I think I agree with you on this one."

"This means I'm bringing you to the dark side. I'm pretty convincing, huh?"

"No." I shook my head. "I just happen to agree on that one topic."

"Okay." He laid on his side and propped his head on his hand. "You start the next question then."

I tried not to stare at the way his body looked so strong yet relaxed as I tried to think of my argument. I searched his walls and focused on a framed poster from a music festival as I recited the facts and my opinions.

"You go to that?" I pointed to the poster before giving him a chance to dispute my argument.

His gaze moved from my face to where I was pointing. "Yeah. I went last year. You ever been?"

"No." I almost laughed. There was no way in hell my parents would have let me go to a music festival.

"You need to live a little."

"I am living," I said defensively.

"Uh huh." He didn't have an ounce of belief in his voice. "What's the last thing you did just for you?"

As I thought about what he said, his question annoyed me. "I don't know. I went to that party last weekend."

"For Theo," he said his name slowly.

"I... I took a nap yesterday." It was a pathetic answer, but it was the only one I could think of.

But his answering grin told me that I was only proving his point.

"I'm going to the lake tomorrow." I crossed my arms.

"For me or for you?"

"For me?" I pointed at my chest. "Do you know how many bets are going on in our class about what you look like under that shirt?"

He opened his mouth to say something, but I kept going.

"I am going to rack up after seeing you in your swim trunks. I'm pretty sure the pot's up to like fifty dollars plus one girl threw in writing someone's paper."

"You're ridiculous." He rolled his eyes and his hand moved to the edge of his t-shirt. "If that's the only reason you're going, I can just take my shirt off now and save you the trouble."

He lifted his shirt, revealing the smallest sliver of tanned skin.

"But..." I pulled my gaze away from the hint of toned abs to look at his face. "It only seems fair that I get to see something in return." He dropped his shirt and ran his hand over his chin that was starting to get a little stubble. "If I make you wait until tomorrow, I'll get to see you in a bikini."

I sucked in a breath at the thought that he'd want to. "Unless I wear my muumuu."

"Do I even want to know what a muumuu is?" He laughed.

"Think loads of fabric, no shape, no skin showing." I wagged my eyebrows at him. "You won't be able to resist me."

"I have no doubt." He ran his hand over his comforter. "But it's supposed to be eighty-five degrees tomorrow. I don't think your muumuu would last too long."

"Damn." I snapped my fingers.

"I guess you'll just have to come up with a new plan."

"To keep me covered?" I asked.

"To keep me from wanting you."

CHAPTER 8

I PULLED into the parking lot that my GPS directed me to. There were trucks upon trucks parked there with boat trailers attached, and I pulled around the lot until I found a spot that looked like it was safe enough to not be in their way.

The lake was the same shade of green as the trees that surrounded it, and the smooth water was begging me to climb in as sweat already clung to my skin. I looked down at my phone to make sure I was at the right place. Easton had texted me the address this morning after I turned down his offer to ride with him.

I didn't want to field Dillon's questions about what the hell I was or wasn't doing with my TA when she saw me climbing into a car with him, but I knew I would have to answer to her tonight when I got home. She was still asleep when I quietly left the dorm this morning.

I spotted a group of guys near a large dock, and it was impossible not to spot Easton even though the guy standing beside him had the exact same shade of hair.

I climbed out of my car and took a deep breath as I grabbed my bag. I should have asked him who was going to be here. I should have done my research, but after him telling me that he wanted me, I couldn't function even if I wanted to.

Easton Cole said he wanted me.

He played it off after he said it. Not because he didn't mean it, but I think because he saw how much him saying it affected me.

Because all I could think about after that moment was how much I wanted him.

When I had gotten home last night, I had shaved every surface of my body and scrubbed my skin like I was getting ready for the Olympics of touchably soft skin.

But when I pulled on my bikini this morning, I was glad I did. I had almost considered running to Target to grab a one-piece, but that was ridiculous. I had always been self-conscious about my body, but suddenly, I felt self-conscious about every inch of skin.

Easton spotted me as I made my way toward the dock, and he smiled as he left his group without a word and made his way toward me.

"That's one hell of a muumuu." He looked down at my tiny blue jean shorts and white tank top, and the way he was looking at my legs was distracting.

I patted my bag that hung at my side. "I brought an extra just in case."

"Uh huh." He reached out and touched his fingers to mine before pulling my hand toward him. "Come meet the guys."

I took a step in his direction as he took a step backward. "Am I the only girl here?"

"Uh." He looked back toward his friends. "Yeah. I didn't really think that through."

I couldn't help but laugh at the concern on his face. "It's fine."

We made our way onto the dock, and three sets of eyes turned in our direction.

"Guys, this is Maddison. Maddison, this is Ben, Oliver, and my brother, Luke." He pointed to each one as he spoke, and I took them in as I nodded my head hello.

Ben was taller than the rest and looked like he worked out at least twenty times a week if the row after row of abs were anything to show for it. He was watching me with a tight smile, and I had a feeling he was more than a little skeptical of me.

Oliver's large smile was the exact opposite though. His smile lit up his face in a way that made me know instantly that I would like him. He was thicker than the others, still muscular, but it was the kind of muscle that came from hard work rather than a gym. I imagined that his hands would be callused and his hugs would be the best you ever had.

Luke felt harder to read. He looked so much like Easton except younger. His hair was the same golden shade of brown and his skin held the same deep tan that could only have been blessed to them by genetics.

"It's nice to meet you." Luke held his hand out in my direction, and I tried to read his face as I slid my hand in his.

"You too."

He was searching my face just as I was searching his. I don't know what he saw there, but he smiled, a smile so like his brother's before letting go of my hand.

Easton's hand pressed against the small of my back. "You ready?"

"To ride on the boat?" I looked up at his face. "Absolutely."

His eyes tightened as dimples popped out on his cheeks. "I was going to let you go first. Get a feel for it."

"Not happening." I patted his chest over his t-shirt and headed in the direction of the boat the others were already climbing in.

Easton moved onto the boat before me and reached his hands out in my direction to help me in. I gripped his shoulders in my hands and his came down on my hips. It was effortless the way he lifted me off the dock and into the boat, but his fingers were demanding as they dug into my skin. I made the mistake of inhaling as my body pressed against his, taking a lungful of that heady scent that was uniquely him.

I wasn't sure if it was due to the water or my attraction to Easton that left me feeling unsteady on my feet as they finally touched the boat. But my head didn't feel any less swimmy as he pinched my tank top between his fingers before tugging on his slightly.

"You going to take this off?" His smirk was so handsome

and playful, and I found myself forgetting why I ever thought the two of us would be a bad idea.

"Tit for tat, Mr. Cole." I took a long lazy look over his t-shirt just as he gripped it in his fingers and lifted it over his head.

A spark of heat lit up my spine as I studied him. He was wickedly handsome, his body only adding to his allure, and I knew that whatever those girls in our class had been betting on paled in comparison to the real thing.

"What did you say?" He threw his t-shirt down on the chair. "Tit for tat?" He nodded his head toward me and I tugged my bag closer to me as I moved to the front of the boat.

I pulled my towel out of my bag and laid it against the white seat. Easton took a seat behind the steering wheel, but I could still feel him watching me. I took my time pulling out my water bottle, sunscreen, snacks, and anything else I could find hiding in the bottom of my bag, and I startled when the loud engine of the boat roared to life.

Easton pushed his fingers through his hair before sliding a hat on backward to keep it out of his face, and I took the opportunity to unbutton my shorts as he began backing the boat away from the dock.

He shifted gears and the boat started forward, and I lifted, just an inch, off the seat and pulled my shorts down my legs. His head visibly dropped with the movement of the fabric against my skin, and I wondered what it would be like to be completely bare in front of him. To have him track my movements with that same intensity when I couldn't hide.

I made quick work of folding my shorts before I slipped my shirt over my head, and I was thankful that my red bikini covered enough to be considered modest. Because every set of eyes on the boat were watching me, but there was only one that mattered.

One hand was gripping the steering wheel as he led us out

into the main channel of the lake and the other was running over his mouth as he tried to hide his smile.

"What?" I tried to call over the sound of the wind whipping past me, but I wasn't sure if he heard me.

"Nothing." He shook his head before letting his eyes roam over me freely. It was intoxicating, the way he looked at me, the way he didn't care that I knew how much he was appreciating me.

There were no false pretenses. No wondering what he was thinking. It was written all over his face.

I turned toward the front of the boat and let the wind kiss my face in rapid succession as I watched the water zip past us. There were a few other boats out on the water, a couple parked with fishing poles dropped in the water, and one that was pulling a tube behind it. There were several houses tucked along the banks of the lake, but they were surrounded by so many trees that they did little to take away from the natural beauty.

I took a deep breath, the indescribable scent of the water mixed with the clean fresh air filled my lungs, and I felt like it was the first deep breath I had taken in days. Years maybe.

The boat curved around a small island, and I held onto the railing as it tilted on its side as it glided through the water.

The rumble of the engine quieted as the boat slowed, and the quiet cove we pulled into looked peaceful as we came to a stop.

"Who's first?" Luke asked as Oliver started unraveling some sort of ski rope.

"I'll go." Easton stood from his chair, but he was making his way toward me. His body was so large that he practically blocked the back of the boat from view, but I knew that his friends were still back there. I knew they were probably listening.

"You going to be okay while I'm in the water?" Easton was talking to me, but his eyes were roaming up my arms and to my shoulders.

"I think I'll survive." I adjusted my sunglasses on my face, and he finally met my gaze. "Surely one of them can put sunscreen on me if I start to burn."

He smiled so wide that I could practically see all of his teeth, and my stomach flipped as he moved toward me.

"I don't think so, freshman." He pulled his hat from his head and placed it on mine. His fingers were gentle as he tucked stray pieces of hair that had been whipping in the wind behind my ears. "That's my job."

"What if I'm burning?" I cocked an eyebrow at him.

"Then put on that extra muumuu you brought." He flicked the bill of my hat before moving toward the back of the boat and grabbing a black life jacket his brother was holding out to him.

I got on my knees so I could watch him as he sat at the back of the boat and strapped the wakeboard onto his feet. The sun was beaming down against my skin, and I let it warm me in a way that nothing else could as Easton stood on the back of the boat with the ski rope in his hands.

His eyes moved to the front of the boat, searching for me, and he winked at me before he twisted to the side and dropped into the water with a loud splash.

"You can move to the back of the boat if you want to watch him?" Ben said as he settled behind the steering wheel.

"Okay." I nodded as I tucked my towel in the floor so it wouldn't blow away.

Oliver took the seat next to Ben, but Luke was already at the back of the boat, watching his brother. I took the seat opposite him and curled up in the seat as I watched Easton bob in the water.

"You ready?" Luke yelled out to his brother which was met with a thumbs up before the boat soared forward with so much speed that I was worried they had just taken Easton's arms off.

But I had no reason to fear. Easton was lifted to the top of the water, and he shook his head to get water out of his eyes as he adjusted his stance.

He was good. Better than good actually.

I had seen plenty of people wakeboard or ski in my lifetime, but Easton made it look completely effortless. He jumped from wake to wake, moving from one side of the boat to the other, and my fingers dug into the soft white vinyl of my seat as he jumped a wake with enough force to completely flip himself in the air.

I laughed as he landed with complete ease, and Luke looked over at me with a big smile on his face. He was watching his brother as intently as I was. I wasn't sure if it was because he was as impressed as I was or because he was making sure he didn't fall. Either way, the smile didn't fall from his lips as he watched him.

He did a few more jumps and flips before he hit a large wake and flipped backward in the air. He managed to spin around completely, but his board clipped the hard edge of the wake and he jerked forward. I was instantly on my knees as he disappeared under the water.

Ben turned the boat on a hard curve, and I spun around to face the front as we pulled back in Easton's direction.

He was floating on his back with a large smile on his face, and I absently wondered if he was ever unhappy. He always seemed so at ease. So carefree and laid back.

"What'd you think?" he asked from the water as the boat came to a stop beside him.

"You." I pointed my finger at him. "You scared the shit out of me."

He threw his head back in laughter, and for the first time in my entire life, I was insanely attracted to the simple sound of a man's laughter.

"You getting in?" He ran his fingers over the water, but I was already shaking my head. "Live a little, freshman."

I smiled as I flipped him the bird and his friends laughed as I moved back to the front of the boat. Oliver started strapping on a life jacket as Easton climbed back into the boat. He was dripping with water, every inch of his skin glistening, and I had to wipe the corner of my mouth to make sure I wasn't drooling as he pulled the life jacket away from his skin.

Ben and Luke were helping Oliver with his board, but Easton's attention was solely on me. He tracked forward like he was on a mission, and I held out my hands to stop him when I read his intentions across his face.

"Don't." I laughed as he pushed against my hands and buried his soaking wet head into my neck.

"Aren't you hot?" He wrapped me in his arms, and the cold wetness of his skin did nothing to cool me off.

"I am." I squirmed against him, and I felt a small shudder rack through his body.

He slid into the seat next to me, his swim trunks wet against my skin, and ran his fingers through his wet hair. My fingers itched to do the same.

"You're next. After Oliver." He nodded his head to the water where Oliver was already getting ready.

Before I could fully shake my head, he chuckled and dipped down to speak beside my ear. "I'll be right there with you. I won't let anything hurt you."

I turned just slightly to look up at him and his lips were only inches away from mine. "I don't know what I'm doing." Not in wakeboarding, and not with him.

"We'll figure it out together." His voice was soft and luring me into him.

My lashes fluttered against my cheeks and a drop of water slid down my chest as it fell from his skin to mine.

"You ready?" Luke's loud voice called out to Oliver, and I blinked my eyes open and searched Easton's.

He looked like he wanted to say something, maybe to tell me how bad of an idea this was, but he didn't get a chance as the boat surged forward and the loud wind drowned out every word that was on the tip of his tongue. His eyes bounced from the back of the boat to me, and I took a deep breath against the deep vibration of my humming body.

He rested his arm behind me, and I let myself settle against him as I turned my head toward where Oliver was currently matching Easton's earlier tricks. I tried to not think about Easton's body pressed against mine. I tried to not let him see how much it affected me. Just that simple press of skin and the way his breath whispered against my neck.

All I could think about was my lips crashing against his, our bodies pressing together, our heavy breaths getting lost in one another.

And the tenseness of Easton's body against mine told me that he was probably thinking about it too.

"Ohh." Ben's voice whipped over the impossible volume of the wind, and I searched the water for Oliver since I had absolutely no idea what just happened to him.

The boat slowed next to him, and Easton shifted in his seat so he could look at me. "You wanna do this?" He nodded his head toward the water, and I didn't regret the decision to nod my head as Easton's face lit up. He stood reaching for my hand, and I placed it in his before he pulled me toward the back of the boat.

He pulled out another life jacket out from under one of the

boat seats and held it out for me to slip my arms into. I could have done it myself. I could have fastened each of the snaps, but there was something about watching his fingers move so close to my skin as he pressed the two ends together. His eyes dragged over my breasts like a physical touch as he closed the life jacket over them.

He took a step back, looking up at my face as he pulled on his own life jacket, then he helped me onto the back of the boat as Luke put the wakeboard in place for me. Easton sat beside me and helped me slide each of my feet into place before tightening them around my ankles.

"You think you can jump or should I push you?" He arched a brow.

I bumped my shoulder into his. "Help me up."

He grinned and did as I said, his hand holding mine as I wobbled with both of my feet attached to the board.

"Okay. I'm not sure." I giggled and looked over at him. "Push me."

Instead, he lifted me against him, my chest pressed against his, the wakeboard hitting against his shins, and he jumped, the two of us hitting the water at the exact same time.

I pushed up to the surface of the water, my feet feeling impossibly heavy in the water, and Easton pushed my hair out of my face before throwing his hat back on the boat. His hand gripped the ski rope as he tread water, and I floated as his feet found mine and he helped me bring the wakeboard forward.

"We're going to take this slow." He pressed the rope in my hand and I gripped it so tightly my knuckles started turning white.

"Okay." I nodded my head even though I was scared to death.

He swam, the lap of water from his movements splashing against me before he settled directly behind me and gripped the rope with me. His feet pushed against the board and I felt him angle it where it should be.

"I'm going to have him go very slowly and drag us just a bit so you can get a feel for this. Keep your arms out in front of you. Bend your knees." The force of his own knees behind mine pushed them where he wanted them. "Try to keep the board at this angle. We don't want the front of the board to dip under the water."

We were plastered together from calves to chest, and his words felt like a caress as he spoke over my shoulder. Suddenly, I was thankful to be in the green water that hid the goosebumps on my skin, but they couldn't hide the way I forced my thighs together to attempt to stop the deep pulse in my sex that felt like it was echoing around us.

His thighs pressed against mine in the same movement, and I shifted, my ass pressing against him. He let out a low groan just as I felt how badly he wanted me as well, and the loud roar of the engine did nothing to deter the way he crept over my skin like a caress.

"You good?" Luke leaned over the back of the boat and called out to us.

"Yeah." Easton's voice was rough and made me crave the sound like a junkie. I pressed against him again, the only thing between us was my small bathing suit bottoms and his trunks, and he whispered, "Shit," just as tension pulled on my arms and we started moving forward.

I was surprised by the force of the water pushing against me as the boat pulled us forward, but Easton helped straighten my wobbling board with his feet.

"Try to keep it steady." His left hand came down on my thigh. "Bend your knees a bit more. It will give you more balance."

"Okay." I nodded and did as he said.

"When they give it more gas, let the boat pull you forward. Don't try to force yourself up."

I nodded my head even though I had no idea what he was talking about.

"Once you're up, let the boat do the work. Your board should be to the side like I was. Relax and go with it."

"That's easy for you to say." I tightened my hands and he chuckled against my neck.

"Keep your weight balanced on your feet and have fun."

"Okay." I nodded, more to myself than him. "I can do this."

I could practically feel him smiling behind me. "You ready?"

"No." The words slipped past my lips as I nodded my head.

Easton's left hand left the rope again, and he lifted his thumb in the air for Luke to see. It was only a moment later when I felt Easton's lips, like a phantom whisper, against my neck then the tension I felt earlier increased tenfold and Easton dropped the rope.

I started to search for him, but my body was lifting out of the water and I could only focus on not dying as my board wobbled against the water.

Getting lifted out of the water wasn't as hard as I had expected, but once I was up, everything that Easton had instructed me went out the window and I stiffened up like my life depended on it. My board hit the rough water and I tugged on the rope to try to balance myself, but it was a mistake. I hit the water face first, the board coming off my feet due to the force, and I surfaced coughing up water.

My arms ached from trying to hold on to the rope, but I couldn't stop laughing as I laid on my back and let the rays of the sun touch my face.

"Are you okay?" I looked to the left to search for the sound of Easton's voice and smiled as he swam toward me.

"I think so," I said the words around laughter as I tried to come down from the adrenaline high.

He tugged on one of the straps of my life jacket, pulling me closer to him, and his gaze ran over me, searching every inch.

"You were amazing." He grinned down at me.

"I fell in the first five seconds." I could see the boat pulling back around us.

"Yeah, but that's five seconds longer than most. A lot of people don't even get up their first time."

"Oh. I can get it up." I snorted at my own joke before it was even fully out of my mouth. My words caught him off guard and his bottom lip slipped between his teeth.

"You're the cutest."

I groaned and pressed my head back against the water. "That's what every girl wants to hear after making a joke about getting it up."

He laughed as his hand snaked around my neck and he pulled me toward him. "What did you want me to say? That I've been thinking about ripping that fucking bikini off you since you shimmied out of those shorts?"

I swallowed my nervousness that was crawling its way up my throat. "That would be a good start," I whispered the words as the boat engine cut off and Luke started reaching over the boat to help me up.

"Dude, your phone's gone off a few times while you were in the water."

"One of your lady friends?" I joked with a raised eyebrow as he pushed me toward the ladder.

"No." Luke chuckled and shook his head. "It said Professor Bryant."

And just like that, the spark left Easton's eyes, the playful banter gone, the easy touches disappeared under the water. I reached for Luke's hand as he helped pull me back into the boat, and I pulled my life jacket off without an ounce of help from Easton.

He could get in trouble for this.

He could get in trouble for me.

I knew that. I knew, but I hadn't cared.

Neither had he.

But I watched him as he climbed into the boat and dropped his life jacket on the ground. He toweled off his face as he picked up his phone and looked over the screen. He had the phone to his ear within the next second, and I moved away from him, back to my spot at the front of the boat.

"Hey, Professor."

I tried not to stare at him while he listened to what the professor was saying, but it was impossible. Regardless of the consequences that were staring us in the face, I still wanted him.

"Yeah." He nodded his head even though the professor couldn't hear him. "That's incredible. Thank you."

He laughed at something he said.

"Yeah. I'm actually out wakeboarding with my friends now." His eyes slid toward me, and I quickly dropped mine and searched my bag for my own phone.

I had two messages, both sent over an hour ago.

Dillon: Where are you?

Theo: Want to hang today?

I quickly replied to Dillon and let her know I would be home in a bit as I listened to and made no sense of Easton's conversation. I clicked on Theo's message.

"No. I'm not slacking on our group project." My eyes jerked back to Easton who was watching me intently. "We actually worked on it yesterday."

I didn't know what the professor had to say about that, but I tried not to think about it. I just typed my reply to Theo letting him know that we could rain check tomorrow. I felt guilty as I typed out the lie that I had a lot of schoolwork, but he would never understand this. He wouldn't accept it.

Whatever the hell this was.

"Alright." Easton ran his fingers through his hair roughly. "I'll see you tomorrow."

He dropped the phone from his ear, and I quickly turned back to mine as a new message from Theo popped up.

Theo: Okay, babe.

It was simple. It was Theo, and it made my stomach turn sour with guilt.

"What'd he want?" Ben asked Easton as he pulled a bottled water out of the small cooler.

"He sent my thesis to a few of his colleagues. He said that a few are interested in meeting with me."

I had never seen Easton seem so unsure of himself, so modest.

"That's awesome." Luke pulled Easton into him and clapped him on the back in a way that only men do. "You should be stoked."

"I am." Easton nodded as if he needed to remind himself.

"What group project is he talking about? You get stuck helping some students?" Oliver laughed, but I didn't.

Did they not know that I was Easton's group project? Did they not know that he was my TA?

Easton's eyes met mine, and I expected him to lie. But his eyes only narrowed slightly before he pointed in my direction. "Maddison is my group project partner."

"Fuck." I heard the word whispered, but I wasn't sure who said it.

"We're discussing The Awakening." His eyes were still on me, and I didn't dare look away from him.

"Are you fucking stupid?"

He finally looked over to his brother, and I pulled my towel around me. I felt so exposed, so on display. Easton and I had been walking a fine line, but we hadn't done anything wrong. We had barely even touched.

"We haven't done anything." He echoed my thoughts.

"Except eye fuck the hell out of each other all day."

I winced at Luke's words and looked out toward the water.

Easton said something back, but I didn't know what it was. His voice was hushed and angry, and I tried to drown them out. I didn't want to hear all their reasons Easton and I didn't work. I already knew them. I was sure that he did too.

I didn't know how long I sat there staring at the still water while they argued in hushed voices, but I was startled when the boat engine started and Easton took the seat directly across from me. His legs were so long that they crowded mine, and when I glanced over at him, I hated the frustrated look on his face.

I watched his profile, the trees in the background nothing but a blur as we passed them. He was beautiful, especially as the sun began to drop and spill a blanket of orange across the sky.

He didn't look at me as Ben pulled the boat back up to the dock or as I gathered my stuff in my bags and said a quick goodbye to all the guys. It felt weird. To have such a great day ruined by such a small moment. Ruined by an idiotic rule.

Easton climbed out of the boat and reached his hand out to me as his eyes finally met mine. I took his hand without an ounce of hesitation and let him pull me up the dock with him. He didn't even acknowledge his friends as he began walking me to my car, and it was the most silent we had been around each other since we had met.

I pressed the unlock button on my keys and turned to him.

"I think I have everything we need for the project. I'll type it up and email it over to you to see what you think."

"Maddison." My name left his mouth like a plea.

"It's fine, Easton." I shook my head and forced a smile on my face. "They're right."

"I need you to understand." He took a small step toward me, and I held my breath.

"I get it." I laughed.

"No." He shook his head. "If I lose my TA position, I lose my scholarship. I could lose any potential scholarships for grad school. Any potential connections that Professor Bryant has."

I opened my mouth to respond, but he kept going.

"If he found out about you, I would lose it. I could lose all of it."

"We haven't done anything wrong." I knew that it was a weak argument as soon as it left my lips.

"I know." He nodded and his fingers brushed over mine. "But I want to."

I didn't know what to say because I did too. Even now, even with him telling me that this couldn't happen, I couldn't stop staring at his mouth. I couldn't stop thinking about what it would be like for him to kiss me.

But I wouldn't do that to him.

"I'll see you in class tomorrow." I opened my car door and put space between us.

He ran his hand through his hair, and I knew he was trying to figure out what to say to me. How to somehow make this better.

But I didn't give him a chance. I climbed into my car and smiled at him before I closed the door. "Goodbye, Easton."

CHAPTER 9

I FOLLOWED Dillon as we squeezed through the student section. There was a red and black game today, but by the look of the crowd, you would think we were playing some huge rival instead of our own team.

Football wasn't something I was normally into, but Theo was starting this year. I didn't miss a single one of his games in high school, and I wasn't planning on starting now.

Because football was everything to him.

I straightened my number seven jersey that matched his and took a seat next to Dillon as we waited for the game to start.

"This is so exciting." Dillon looked around at the sea of students who were all dressed in red and black. I noticed several of them from Theo's fraternity, some even waving at me as we saw each other. "Have you ever been to a college game before?"

"Yeah." I pointed to the right toward the fifty-yard line. "My parents have season tickets right over there."

"They big fans?"

I laughed. "That's an understatement. My dad played when he went to college here, and I think he thinks they'll lose if he doesn't come to every single game."

She laughed as if I was laughing, but I wasn't. "What about your mom?"

"She's a fan too." My mother was always a fan of anything my father liked.

"That's so cool. My parents are more into games like Monopoly." She chuckled like she was embarrassed.

"That sounds amazing, actually. I'd much rather play a good board game."

She looked over at me with a smile. "You look like the board game type."

I reached my hand into her popcorn and popped some in my mouth. "I will take that as a compliment."

"You should."

Everyone around us started to cheer as the team ran onto the field. Dillon and I joined them on our feet, and it took me a few minutes to spot the number seven plastered across Theo's chest.

He took the field in a black jersey, and I waved at him as if he could somehow spot me within all the other students.

I knew that he was anxious to prove himself today. But he didn't need to worry. The very first play, the ball was thrown to Theo, and he caught the ball with ease and took off down the field before being tackled. Twenty yards. It wasn't a bad start.

"Go, Theo!" I cupped my hands around my mouth and yelled, even though I knew he couldn't hear me.

"What's the deal with you two anyway?" Dillon asked as she watched me.

"What deal?" I knew exactly what she was asking, but I didn't want to answer her. I didn't know how to answer her.

"You and Theo. Are you two fucking or something?"

I shoved her shoulder, and she grinned.

"No. We're not fucking. We're friends."

"But you want to fuck him." She said the words like she was so sure.

"Is that a question?"

"I don't know. Is it?"

I rolled my eyes at her and turned back to the game. Theo had the football again, but I missed half the play due to Dillon.

"He's been my best friend for years." I looked over at her then back at the game.

"As you've said." She nodded her head. "What I'm asking is do you want to fuck your best friend?"

I tightened my ponytail on top of my head. "You're nosey. Has anyone ever told you that?" If she had asked me the question a couple weeks ago, it would have been a clear cut answer.

Yes. Yes, I wanted to fuck him. Yes, I wanted more from him. Yes to everything, but now I wasn't so sure.

"All the time." She wrapped her arm around my shoulder. "But I'm going to help you get from the friend zone to the end zone."

I couldn't help it. Laughter bubbled out of me at her lame joke.

"Get it? It's a football reference."

"I got it." I shoved my elbow into her side. "But this is not some get Maddison laid mission. Theo means more to me than that."

"I know he does." She leaned her head against mine. "I just wanted to hear you admit that you wanted him out loud."

I almost told her then that it wasn't Theo I couldn't get out of my head, but I couldn't say those words out loud. If I did, then it would somehow make it more real. I hadn't even seen Easton since my class on Monday. A class where he managed to not look at me for the entirety of the lecture.

I shouldn't have let it bothered me, but it did. It pissed me off.

What pissed me off more was that I couldn't stop looking at him.

"Excuse me." A girl was trying to get past us, and I turned to the side to let her through.

And I saw him.

Easton was sitting two rows behind us with Ben and Oliver, and I watched him laugh with his friends before I jerked my attention back forward and tried to calm my racing heart.

"You okay?" Dillon looked over at me like I was crazy.

"Yeah. I'm good." I pulled on the frayed edge of my shorts. "Perfect actually."

She narrowed her eyes at me before she turned her head to

search the crowd. I snatched her hand in mine, and she turned her direction back to me.

"What's wrong?"

"Just give me a second, and I'll tell you." I stared toward the game, but I wasn't seeing any of it.

"You know my group project partner?" I was whispering the words to her like he could somehow overhear me from two rows back.

"The older TA?" She wagged her eyebrows. "Yeah. What about him?"

"He's here."

She started to turn again, but I squeezed her hand in mine. "Okay. So, why are you acting weird?"

What was I supposed to tell her? That I was insanely attracted to him, but now he was avoiding me like I was a stage five clinger?

"Oh my God." She inhaled loudly. "Did you sleep with him?"

"No." I shook my head and peeked behind me. I turned back around quickly and cursed under my breath. He was staring directly at me.

"Which one is he?"

I knew if I didn't tell her she was going to embarrass the hell out of me.

"He's two rows behind us. Dark brown hair. He's wearing a black t-shirt and jeans."

She glanced over her shoulder inconspicuously, but her jaw was practically on the ground when she turned back toward me.

"The one staring at you?" she whisper-yelled at me.

I glanced back in his direction and our gazes finally met, and I felt like everything else around us was just static. Because no matter how hard I tried, I couldn't look away.

The crowd around us erupted in cheers, and Oliver smacked Easton's shoulder in excitement. His eyes glanced in his direction, and I quickly turned back around while I had the chance.

"Holy shit." Dillon fanned herself. "Are you about to spontaneously combust?"

I rolled my eyes at her and tried to remember why I was there. I searched the field for Theo.

"I'm serious. He was just looking at you like he wants to eat you alive. Like he would do it right here with everyone watching."

I finally found number seven, and I watched him as he lined up in formation. "Let me assure you, that is not the case."

"What is the case then?" She angled her head to look at me.

"He's my TA." I tried to say the words with a sense of finality so maybe I would start to believe them too.

"Okay?" She let the word drag across her lips.

"And he can get in trouble."

"Not that much trouble. I heard TAs barely make any money anyway." She glanced back again before looking at me. "Plus, he doesn't look like he got the memo."

"He's the one who gave it to me."

"Oh." She winced like she could physically feel the sting of my rejection.

"He could lose his scholarship if he loses his TA position." I needed to repeat that statement over and over again in my head.

"Fuck."

"Yeah." I nodded in agreement. "So, I just have to keep my distance from him."

She narrowed her eyes at me. "That's your grand plan. Avoid him and then rub one out to his gorgeous face?"

I smacked her arm and she laughed. "What? That's what

I'd be doing if I were you. Just put a sock on the door so I know."

"You are ridiculous." I stole another handful of her popcorn and shoved it in my mouth.

"And you're insane if you think you're going to be able to ignore all that." She peeked over her shoulder again. "Especially with the way he's looking at you. I would be up there dry humping him right now if I was you."

The crowd cheered again, and this time, I watched as Theo caught the ball and ran a few feet for a touchdown.

"Wooo," I yelled and clapped my hands and tried not to think about what Easton was doing behind me.

Theo's "team" was up by fourteen points, and I couldn't stop smiling as him and one of his teammates bumped chests in celebration.

"Which one do you want more?" Dillon asked as she watched me.

"What?" I was still clapping with everyone else as I looked over at her.

"Which one do you want to dick you down more? Theo or Easton?"

"Did you really just say dick you down?"

"I did." She nodded, clearly proud of herself.

"Have I told you that you are bat shit crazy today?"

"You have." She shrugged her shoulders. "But you still didn't answer my question."

I looked back out toward the game. "Because I'm not going to."

"Interesting." She tapped her chin dramatically. "I wonder if it's because you don't want to answer or if it's because you don't know the answer yourself."

I rolled my eyes and ignored her. Partly because she was getting on my nerves and partly because she was right. Not the part about being dicked down, but the part where I had no clue what I wanted.

I managed to only look back toward Easton three more times during the game, and only one of those times, he was looking back at me. I tried not to do it at all, but there was a feeling in my tummy, a deep tingle in my spine, knowing that he was behind me. No matter how much I told myself that I didn't care, I couldn't stop.

Once the game ended, I quickly moved toward the field with Dillon. I glanced back once at Easton. He was talking to a group of guys who sat near him in the bleachers, and I'd be lying if I said that I hated that I couldn't hear the sound of his laugh as he threw his head back in laughter.

The players were all on the field talking. Some were high-fiving, some looked pissed, but Theo had his head down and was listening to something one of the coaches was saying to him.

I waved at him once he finally looked up, and he grinned when he spotted me. His coach clapped him on his shoulder pads then he moved in my direction. There was a good five or six feet that still separated the bleachers to where he stood, but I could see the droplets of sweat as they slipped down his face.

"Good game." I smiled at him to match the one on his face.

"Thank you." He nodded toward Dillon before bringing his attention back to me. "That's a nice looking jersey you have there."

I looked down at the number seven plastered across my chest that matched his. "I have to represent the best damn player on the field." I thumped my fist against my chest twice like I was some sort of gang member.

But Theo laughed, his brown eyes squinting from the force of his cheeks.

One of the players clapped him on the back as he passed

and said something I couldn't make out, but Theo nodded his head.

"I have to head to the locker room. You're going to be at the party, right?"

I hadn't planned on going. I had planned on avoiding that frat house like the plague, but Theo's face looked so hopeful as he asked the question and I had never learned how to tell him no.

"We'll be there." I leaned over the rail a bit and found myself wanting to touch him.

"Keep the jersey on." He winked at me. "It looks hot on you."

With that, he took off in the direction of the locker room, and I was left more confused than ever.

CHAPTER 10

THE FRAT HOUSE was completely packed as usual as Dillon and I walked in. Everyone was excited. It was the first football game of the season, even if it was against our own team, and the energy was electric.

There was more red and black than I had ever seen filling the walls of the house, and I wasn't surprised to see the guys whose chests were completely covered in chipping black and red paint manning the keg.

I hopped up onto the counter as Dillon started pouring herself a drink from the selection of liquor, and I watched people as they high fived players as they strolled in like they were some kind of gods. Drinks were put into their hands without them even asking, girls were attached to their hips like leeches, and I swear, people moved just to let them walk by.

Theo had texted me ten minutes ago to let me know he would be at the house soon. I probably should have waited for him, but we didn't. Instead, Dillon was shoving a plastic cup in my hand that had her latest concoction in it, and I took a long drag to try to calm my racing thoughts.

"Hi."

I looked up at the guy standing in front of me. He was cute, in an adorably nerdy way, and I found myself smiling at him.

"Hi."

"I'm Brett. I think you're in my math class."

"Oh yeah." I snapped my fingers. "Sorry. I can barely understand a thing that man says, so it's hard to remember faces of the people in there."

He laughed, but I was sure he didn't have any trouble understanding any of it. "You're Maddison, right?"

"Right." I nodded my head and leaned forward on the counter a bit. My hands were resting on the edge and my feet were dangling in front of me.

"If you ever need help, I'm pretty good at math," he said shyly, and I knew that this was the kind of guy I should be looking for. A sweet, uncomplicated guy who could like me, who did like me, without any problems.

"Are you hitting on my girl?"

The question came at the same time I was about to tell him thank you, but Brett physically shrunk away from me as Theo leaned against the counter.

"Don't be an ass, Theo." I shoved my shoulder into his. "Thank you, Brett. I might just have to take you up on that."

"No problem." He muttered the words before he turned and moved away from us without a second thought.

Theo smiled up at me, but I shoved his shoulder again.

"That was rude."

"Oh come on." He rolled his eyes. "That guy didn't have a chance with you anyway." He turned his body to face me, and even though I was struck with how handsome he was, his comment pissed me off.

"You don't know that." I shook my head and tightened my fingers around the counter. "I could have been interested in him."

He moved in front of me and pressed his hands against my knees. "I'm sorry. Alright?" His grin told me that he wasn't actually sorry at all. "I think I would know if you were into someone."

I should have told him that he was wrong. I should have told him that he hadn't been able to see that I was into someone for the last five years, but I couldn't. I had the same argument in my head so many times before—whether it was worth it or not, but it never seemed to be. The consequences always seemed to steep. Risking our friendship for the chance at something more. It was too treacherous.

"Yeah." I nodded my head with a smile on my face. The same smile I always gave him when it came to us. The same smile I had mastered years before.

Dillon tapped her finger against my thigh, and she sipped her drink as she inconspicuously nodded her head toward the kitchen entrance.

I heard the sound of his voice before I saw him. He was joking around with someone behind him, and my breath caught in my throat.

I honestly didn't think Easton showed up to things like this. I had never seen him at a party before when I came with Theo, but here he was.

From my vantage point on the counter, I watched him walk into the kitchen and grab a plastic cup from one of the guys at the keg. He hadn't noticed me, and I wasn't positive that I wanted him to.

Because I couldn't look at him without wanting to kiss him, and I knew that he couldn't look at me without knowing.

"Theo, you in for a game of beer pong?" one of Theo's frat brothers yelled through the open patio door.

"Yeah." His hand gently squeezed my thigh. "I'll be right there."

"You going to come outside and cheer me on." His body was settled in between my thighs as he spoke to me, and I hadn't even thought about our position until I looked up and saw Easton watching us.

I forced myself to look away from Easton and the daggers he was staring into Theo's back. "Yeah. I'll be out there in a few. I need to use the bathroom first."

"Okay." He reached forward and tucked a stray piece of hair behind my ear. "I'll see you out there."

He moved away from me, the loss of his warmth instant. I

tried not to immediately look in Easton's direction, but it was impossible.

I wondered if those around him, those that got to be near him, that got to hear his laugh and see the deep creases of his dimples, knew how lucky they were.

But he wasn't looking at them. He was watching me.

And he was savagely seducing me without a single touch. His gaze was physical, like a burning caress, and I knew that if I didn't protect myself, I was going to become addicted to something I could never have.

I jumped off the counter and turned toward Dillon. "I'm going to run to the bathroom real quick. I'll meet you outside."

She nodded, already turning back to her conversation with some guy I have never seen before I walked away.

I could feel Easton tracking my every move as I pushed through the crowd of people to get to the bathroom, but I didn't stop. I stared ahead as I moved past him, and I guess God thought I finally deserved a bit of luck, because I actually found the bathroom open.

I closed the door, the loud click echoing off the nearly silent bathroom walls, and I pressed my back to the door.

My body felt like it was on fire, my blood rushing through my veins, my heart electric with confusion. I turned my head to the side and stared at myself in the mirror. My hair was a wild mess of waves on the top of my head, my cheeks were flushed, and Theo's number seven sat on my chest like a brand.

I inhaled, as deeply as I could, before blowing out a slow breath. It was only weeks ago that I knew exactly where I stood. I was the undecided freshman who was best friends with the star football player and the daughter of what seemed like the perfect parents. I knew what was expected of me. I knew what I was supposed to do.

But everything seemed like it was turned up on its head.

I turned on the water as cold as it would go, and I ran my fingers through the cascade. I needed to forget about Easton. While he made it perfectly clear that we were off limits, the way he looked at me was messing with my head.

But I didn't have time for any more boys who didn't know what they wanted from me.

I quickly dried my hands and tightened my ponytail.

I was here to be with Theo, to celebrate with Theo, and that was what I was going to do.

I pulled the door open and braced myself for what I knew laid behind it, but I stopped short at the sight of Easton leaning against the wall.

"We have to stop meeting like this." His hands were tucked in his pockets, and I would have thought he was relaxed if it wasn't for that tiny hitch in his smile.

"I'm starting to think you're following me." I arched an eyebrow at him, and his smile finally turned genuine.

"It would seem that way, huh?"

He was beyond confusing.

"Well, if you'll excuse me. I need to get back to Theo."

He moved then, his body blocking my escape, and I made the mistake of breathing in the smell of him.

"Why him?" He asked the question like it was the easiest thing in the world to answer.

"What do you mean?" I looked up into his eyes. "Why not him?"

He pulled his bottom lip between his teeth, and I could tell he was warring with himself about what he wanted to say.

"Why not him?" I repeated the question slowly.

"He doesn't deserve you."

I couldn't help but laugh. He didn't know a thing about Theo. He didn't have a clue what he deserved.

"Who does deserve me then, Easton?" I threw my hands

out to my sides. "If Theo doesn't deserve me and you don't want me, then who?"

He stepped closer to me, closing the space between us, but I took a matching step back.

"I never said I didn't want you."

"No." I shook my head. "You said you can't have me. You're my TA, remember? They don't get to determine who I date either."

His eyes burned against mine. "Are you and Theo dating now?"

"What if we are?" I didn't know why I was pushing him, but there was something about it that felt good. Getting a reaction out of him, provoking him.

"You're wearing his jersey." His eyes roamed over my chest.

"I am." I nodded my head.

"I fucking hate it." He moved toward me again, and this time, I let him.

His hand slid around my back pulling me into his body, and I barely managed to breathe out the words, "You're my TA."

"I don't care." His words were quick and sure, and he didn't hesitate as his mouth dropped to mine and he kissed me. There was no warning, no permission, he simply pressed his lips to mine and drew out my ragged breath as if it belonged to him.

His hand pressed against the back of my neck, angling me exactly where he wanted me, and my heart paused for what seemed like an eternity before his tongue caressed the seam of my lips. The small amount of fight I had in me disappeared, and I gripped his arms beneath my fingertips as I tried to hold onto him with everything I had.

His tongue met mine, wild and unrestrained, and I wrapped my legs around his waist as he lifted me in the air and placed me down on the counter. I heard the door shut behind him, but I didn't dare look up. Instead, I tightened my legs around him and groaned into his mouth as his groin pressed against mine.

"Fuck," he whispered the word against my lips before his mouth moved down the curve of my neck. The heat of his breath warmed my skin while leaving a trail of chill bumps on every inch that went untouched. I arched into him, desperate for more, but a loud knock on the door caused me to jump and his lips to slip from my skin.

"Just a second," his gruff voice called out to whoever was on the other side of the door, and I tried to catch my breath as I felt the rapid push and pull of his on my skin.

"I should get outside anyway before Theo starts looking for me." I hated saying those words to him, but they were true. Theo would come looking for me.

He pushed away from me, just slightly, so he could look down at me, and I practically purred as he ran his fingers along my jaw until they stroked the sensitive skin of my lips.

"Don't run back to him."

"I'm not." I shook my head. "He's my best friend."

He nodded his head, but he didn't look convinced.

"Meet me at the library tomorrow." I couldn't leave this bathroom without knowing he didn't think this was a mistake. I needed to know that I was going to see him. "We can finish up our project."

"Just the project, huh?" He arched a brow at me, and my stomach flipped at the way he smiled.

"Who knows what could happen in the library?" I pushed against his chest and climbed off the counter. "That place holds all the secrets."

He caught my chin in his hand. "Until tomorrow, then?"

I licked my lips and tried to think about how I would survive until tomorrow without kissing him again.

"Until tomorrow."

He pressed his lips against mine, softer than earlier, but too rough to be called anything but vital. He looked me over one last time, his eyes saying more than he was, then he opened the bathroom door.

CHAPTER 11

I DIDN'T SEE much of Easton the rest of the night. I joined Theo while he won his game of beer pong, and this time when he asked me to stay the night, I turned him down.

I didn't want to sleep in Theo's bed when I couldn't stop thinking about Easton.

The library was relatively dead when I walked in the next day. To say that I was anxious to see Easton was an understatement. I hadn't told Dillon about our kiss. I didn't want her to make more out of it than it was. Especially when I had no clue what was happening myself.

Easton was clear that day at the lake that he couldn't be anything with me, but last night was more than confusing. It was everything.

Easton was already sitting at a table when I entered, the same table I had sat at last time, and I couldn't stop smiling thinking that maybe he was as anxious to see me as I was him.

"Hi." I set my bag down on the desk in front of him, and he looked relieved when he looked up. Like maybe he thought I wouldn't come.

"Hi." He ran his fingers through his hair and smiled as I sat down across from him.

We stared at each other, neither of us knowing what to say, before we both opened our mouths at the same time.

"I got you something." Easton pulled his backpack off of the chair beside him and set it on the table.

"It was a pretty good first kiss, but I didn't know we were doing gifts," I joked.

He cocked an eyebrow at me. "Just pretty good?"

"I don't know." I shrugged my shoulders. "It was at least in my top five."

I was lying and we both knew it. It was the best kiss I had in my entire life.

"I guess I'll just have to try harder next time, huh?" He unzipped his backpack and started rummaging through it.

"That would be my suggestion, and I wouldn't stop until I got that number one spot."

He pulled a black case out of his backpack and set it in front of me. "I bought this before our mediocre kiss." He smiled, but he looked nervous.

"What is it?" I had no idea what he could have bought me. Honestly, we barely knew each other.

"Open it." He nodded in the direction of the box.

I pulled the box closer to me and lifted the lid without an ounce of patience. I stared at the present that laid inside.

"Do you hate it?" Easton shifted in his seat, but I didn't look up at him. I was too busy staring at the camera. "If you don't like it, you don't have to keep it."

I pulled the box a couple inches closer to me so he wouldn't take it away from me.

"Why?" That simple, complicated word slipped past my lips.

"Why what?" I finally looked up at him, and he was looking over every inch of me. "You said this is what you love. It's not brand new." He reached for the box and pulled it out. "A friend of mine was selling his online, so I bought it."

He said it so simply like he hadn't just given me the most thoughtful gift ever.

He pushed the camera into my hands, and I hesitantly took it. "This is too much."

"It's not." He chuckled softly. "It's not a big deal."

But it was. It was a huge freaking deal.

"Now you can practice your photojournalism, and maybe you'll decide that it is the right major for you."

I was shaking my head as he said the words because I couldn't. I had already made the decision to put it out of my head. My parents wanted me to get a business degree like my father.

But it felt like the last thing I wanted.

"I was accepted to Columbia." I looked up at him as I said the words I wasn't even meaning to say.

"What?" He almost looked shocked, but I couldn't say that I blamed him.

"I did." I nodded my head. "I wrote this entrance essay, and I took photos on my phone that I included. They offered me a scholarship."

"What happened?"

It was almost embarrassing to answer him, almost shameful.

"I came here instead."

He watched me as if he was searching for the answer, as if he could find the truth resting on my face. "Because of your parents?"

"Yeah." I nodded. "But it was more than that. Because of Theo."

I waited for his reaction, but he hid it well. Instead of what I expected him to do, he turned his head to the side and watched me.

"He mean that much to you?"

It felt weird talking about Theo with him like this.

"I told you he's my best friend, but it's what's expected of me. My parents went here. My dad wants me to work for him when I graduate."

"That's a lot of what other people want."

I didn't reply because I didn't know what I would say. Yes. I was letting my parents control my future. That I got a scholarship to Columbia, but my dad said he wouldn't pay for my living expenses. It sounded weak, and it made me feel weak.

"Thank you for this." I hugged the camera closer to my chest. "Seriously, it's amazing."

"You're welcome." He finally smiled. "If you need a practice subject, just let me know." He flexed his biceps in the air and kissed his right one.

I snorted and clicked the camera on. "I can't believe you just did that."

"Yeah." He laughed with me. "I could feel the douchebag coming out of me as I did it."

I held the camera up to my face and looked at him through the lens.

"What do we still need to work on for the group project?" I snapped a picture of him as he spoke.

"Nothing." I looked down at the camera and viewed the photograph. He was almost as handsome on the screen as he was in person. "I finished typing it up yesterday. You can read it if you want."

"So, this was just a ploy to get me here?" He stood from his chair and started moving around the table toward me.

"You could say that."

"Well." He stuck his hand out to me. "Let's go take some photos."

We moved through the library stacks, and I laughed as Easton grabbed my hand and pulled me around the corner. He twisted me around, pressing my back to his chest, and he held the camera out in front of us, snapping a quick selfie.

He put the camera back in my hand, and I almost dropped it when he pressed his lips against my neck.

He moved through another stack of books, and I followed him with my camera as we seemed to move farther away from everyone. I snapped a photo of him as he walked, his face turned back toward me, laughter evident on every line of his face.

"What are you doing?" I whispered because I didn't want to get in trouble with the librarians. They seemed harmless enough, but I knew better than to underestimate the quiet ones.

He disappeared around another corner, and I struggled to keep up with him. I rounded the corner he had just taken and I squealed as his arms wrapped around my waist and lifted me in the air.

"Shhh..." He laughed as he whispered against my lips, but I couldn't stop giggling. Easton was too much. He made me feel too good, and I wasn't naive enough to realize how badly that scared me.

Easton's hand wrapped around the back of my head before he fully pressed his lips to mine. I leaned into him, pushing him back against the shelf, and a few books fell to the floor in a loud clatter.

"Shhh." Easton laughed and quickly squatted down to grab the books. "You're going to get us in trouble."

I could feel my skin blossoming with heat, and it didn't matter that we were in the middle of our school library. I wanted him.

"Maybe I want a little trouble."

He stared at me so boldly and intimately that I felt like I was on fire. I had never been looked at like that before.

He opened his mouth, I hoped to say that he wanted it too, but the next words I heard weren't his.

"This is a library. Not a sex pit."

Easton and I both looked over at the librarian, and even though I tried, I couldn't stop the snort that echoed through the room as I tried to rein in my laughter.

She turned her attention fully to me, and even though I knew I should have been worried about being caught. I couldn't stop laughing.

"What's your name?" She took a step toward me, but Easton blocked her path.

"We were just leaving." His words were said with their own edge of laughter, and it only seemed to fuel mine. He pushed me in the opposite direction of the librarian, moving us quickly through the aisles, and we clung to each other as we pushed out the library door into the fresh air.

"I didn't give you enough credit, freshman." He looked me up and down as he laughed. "You have more balls than I thought."

CHAPTER 12

"WE'RE NOT WATCHING this movie again." I groaned from Theo's bed as he set up the TV.

"*The Fast and the Furious* is a fucking classic." He looked affronted that I would think anything different.

"Yeah because it's so dang old." I popped some chocolate covered raisins in my mouth. "Like you."

"I don't know who you're calling old. You're only a year younger than me."

"Yes." I winked at him. "But I will always be a year younger."

He grabbed his remote and plopped down on the bed beside me. "I remember when you used to hate that you were younger than me. I got my permit first, my license first. I had to buy your tickets to R-rated movies."

"True." I stuffed a pillow behind my head and leaned back. "Do you remember that time we watched *Transformers* then sneaked into *The Fault in Our Stars*?"

"Yeah." He chuckled. "You were a bad influence."

"Me?" I pointed to my chest. "I'm pretty sure that you're the one who talked me into that."

"No. I remember specifically that you threw a fit because we were watching *Transformers* so I had to sneak us into *The Fault in Our Stars* to make it up to you. I don't think I've ever seen you cry so hard."

"That's a sad freaking movie." I tried to defend myself. "But it's so beautiful and so perfect. Let's watch it instead of *The Fast and the Furious*."

"No way." He shook his head, hard and fast. "I barely survived that movie with you once. There's no way in hell I would do it again."

I pouted, but he just smiled as he pressed play on a movie I knew he had seen at least a hundred times before.

But it made him happy, and I loved seeing him happy. So I

put away my puppy dog eyes and watched the movie. If nothing else, there was plenty of eye candy, and I was with my best friend.

Theo was passed out completely as the movie continued to play. I shoved him, but he didn't even budge. I checked the time on my phone. It was only ten forty-five, and I was nowhere near sleepy.

I pressed Easton's name on my phone and my fingers hovered over the keys.

Theo's profile bounced in and out of view through the TV light. He looked so peaceful, and I knew that I shouldn't leave him. But I pressed my finger against my phone anyway.

What are you doing?

Easton: Reading. You?

Are you in your room?

Easton: Yes. Are you here?

I didn't give it much more thought as I slowly climbed out of Theo's bed, trying my best not to disturb him, and crossed the room. I tried not to look back at his face as I turned the handle and slipped out into the bright hallway.

I quickly made my way to Easton's door and rapped my knuckles against it. I could hear movement behind his door, and it only took a few seconds before he pulled it open.

I tightened my hands behind my back and ogled at what stood in front of me. He was wearing a pair of red flannel pajamas that were slung low on his hips and no shirt covered his drool-worthy abs.

"Hi."

I finally looked up at his smiling face. "Hi."

He still had a book in his hand. I couldn't make out what it was, but it was old and tattered at the edges.

"What are you doing here?" He looked down the hallway.

"I'm staying the night with Theo."

His eyes darkened, but he didn't say anything about it. "His room is down there." He nodded in the direction of Theo's door.

"I know." I shifted my feet.

"But you're here." It wasn't a question. Or maybe it was. Either way, he knew that I was here instead of where I should have been with Theo.

"Are you going to invite me in?"

He stepped back out of the doorway and waved his hand in the direction of his room with a grin on his face.

He was clearly in bed getting ready for sleep because his bed was in disarray and the only flicker of light through the room was provided by the lamp beside his bed. He shut the door behind him as I stepped into his space.

"I didn't mean to interrupt you." I pointed to his book. "I just wanted see you for a minute."

He stepped toward me, backing me up toward his bed, and grinned. "I'm glad you did." He was staring at my lips as he said the words.

"Yeah?" I watched as his tongue peeked out and wet his bottom lip.

He didn't answer me. At least not with words. Instead, he closed the small space between us and thrust his fingers in my hair without warning. His mouth was against mine, more practiced than the last time, but no less hungry.

I let him lead me, his tongue pushing against mine, his hands tight in my hair, and I didn't stop him when he took one more small step forward and the back of my knees hit the bed. He laid me down slowly, his body hovering over mine, and I was aching for him to drop his weight against me.

His knee was pressed against the bed between my thighs, and I arched up into him, begging his hands to move somewhere other than my hair. He groaned into my mouth as my breasts pushed against his chest and my core pressed against his knee. That one sound seemed to fuel me.

I wasn't a virgin, but I knew that Easton had to be more experienced than I was. But I didn't care about any of that. All that mattered was him touching me.

He tore his mouth away from mine, and I mewled as his lips moved along my jaw before dropping down my sensitive neck. He wasn't gentle. It was as if all his restraint was spent on his body and there was none left when it came to his mouth. His teeth nipped, his tongue caressed, and I was so wet that I didn't know how much more I could take.

"Please, Easton," I cried softly. I didn't even know what I was asking for. I just knew that I needed more.

He pushed my t-shirt up my stomach and his mouth dropped to the soft flesh. Nothing beyond my stomach was exposed, but the way his tongue swirled around my belly button before taking a small bite of my hip made me feel like I was completely bare before him.

My fingers drug through his hair, silently asking him for more, but I could feel his lips hesitating. He lifted his head and looked up at me.

"We should slow down."

I shook my head and gripped tighter in his hair. "Please."

"What do you want, Maddison?" His voice was rougher than I had ever heard it.

"Everything."

He squeezed his eyes closed like I was physically paining him. "Not tonight."

I opened my mouth to object, but he stopped me.

"There's no rush."

I knew what he was saying was true, but it didn't make me want him any less. I let my hand roam over his side until I reached the edge of his pajama pants. "Can I touch you?" I looked up into his eyes. "I want to touch you."

"Fuck." The word was a curse from his lips as his forehead hit my chest.

But he didn't stop me.

His stomach tightened as I hooked one finger beneath the band of his pajamas then moved my hand completely below them. His breath caught in his lungs as I gripped his cock in my hand. It was warm and silky and so hard against my fingers. I wrapped my hand around him, slowly moving my hand up and down, and his breath rushed out against my neck.

He pushed my shirt up, his hands rushed and excited, and exposed my breasts. His hands traced the swell of my breasts above my bra.

I pumped my hand faster, matching the push and pull of his ragged breath, and his teasing touch turned needy. He jerked my bra down, baring my breasts to him, and his thumbs grazed my nipples.

I pressed my thumb to the head of him, and I moaned as his head lowered and pulled my nipple into his mouth. He was as rough there as he had been with my neck, and I could barely control the speed of my hand as my body begged him for more.

He pushed his hands under my pajama shorts and panties, his fingers sliding through me, and he groaned against my breast as he felt my arousal. His finger slid into me with ease as the palm of his hand put pressure on my clit, and I was embarrassed by how quickly my body tightened up around him.

"Easton." His name was a plea—a plea for more, for him to never stop, and it only seemed to fuel him further.

His teeth bit down on my nipple as the pressure from his hand intensified, and I followed the speed of his fingers with mine as we both chased our orgasm.

"Fuck, Maddison." He cried out my name just as I felt his

release hit my hand, and I couldn't hold myself together any longer.

I fell apart around his hand. My back arched into his chest and my mouth found his. He kissed me as he milked out my orgasm.

He pressed his forehead to mine, his breath mingling with my own, and I tried to calm my racing heart that I knew matched his.

"That had to be better than your book." My words were breathy and languid, but they caused his body to shake against mine in laughter.

He dropped his weight beside me and pushed my hair out of my face. "You're kind of a dork. Do you know that?"

"I've been told that a time or two." I pulled my bra back in place before lowering my t-shirt and turning toward him.

He wrapped his arms around me and pulled me into his chest. I could hear the loud steady beat of his heart as he ran his fingers over the back of my head, and I traced the deep ridge of his collarbone with my own.

"Does Theo know you're in here?" His voice sounded like it was the absolute last thing he wanted to talk about, and I couldn't blame him.

Just hearing his name make my chest ache.

I shook my head against him and pressed in tighter.

"I should probably get back before he wakes up and freaks out when I'm missing."

His hand didn't stop his slow, gentle caress over my hair, but he nodded his head in understanding.

"I'll walk you back."

I pushed against his chest as I sat up and looked at him. "Do you think that's the best idea? I don't want this to be the way he finds out about us."

"Do you think he's going to care?" His eyes narrowed slightly, but that was the most he would let his irritation show.

"I don't know what he's going to think, honestly, but I don't think he'd appreciate that I snuck out of his bed to come in here with you."

"Then why did you do it?"

"Because." I pressed my lips gently against his. "I wanted to. I wanted to see you."

He nuzzled his nose into my neck, and I felt his deep inhale of breath as if he was trying to memorize the smell of me.

"Then I'll walk you back."

I didn't argue this time. Instead, I let him hold me against him before we climbed out of bed and he cleaned himself up. I watched his every move as he moved about his room. He was comfortable and confident here, more so than anywhere else, and I loved watching him.

"You ready?" His hand was on the door handle, and I nodded just before he turned it.

We stepped into the hall, him still wearing nothing but his pajama pants, and I was thankful that we were the only two. It was a quick few steps to Theo's room, and I suddenly felt self-conscious as we made it to his door.

"I'll text you tomorrow." Easton rested his hand on Theo's door frame, and I couldn't decide where to look.

"Okay." I nodded and gripped Theo's door handle in my hand. The door creaked open, making the smallest groan as the wood moved forward, and Easton's hand gripped my chin before I could go any farther.

He kissed me. His lips were gentle against mine, but they said more than everything that had just happened in his bedroom.

I was his, and me going back to Theo's room didn't change anything.

CHAPTER 13

"I SWEAR you eat more than anyone I know." Easton laughed as I shoved another bite of lo mein in my mouth.

We had hung out for the last two days. Always in different places, not his room or mine, and I was dying of sexual frustration.

"You're the one who introduced me to this place." I licked some sauce off my phone. "If I can't fit in my jeans anymore, I'm blaming you."

He pushed the plate of eggrolls in my direction. "Trust me. Your jeans are looking perfect."

I rolled my eyes even though my stomach went all gooey at his compliment.

"Based on the pictures you took of me, that must be your favorite part."

He smiled and took another bite of his food without answering.

We had spent the day yesterday taking photos. He didn't complain once as I watched different people throughout our town and snapped pictures of things that moved me. The only thing he photographed that moved him was my ass.

Or my lips.

There were several of those too, and in each one, they were swollen from kissing.

"What do you want to do today?"

"I don't know." I shrugged. My classes were over for the day and the only thing I had been able to think about the entire time was him. "We could go back to my dorm." I wagged my eyebrows.

He grinned, but I knew he would say no. He told me that he wanted to take things slow—that he didn't need all that to be with me, but I was over taking things slow.

"Maddy."

I looked up from my food at the sound of Theo's voice, and

it was instantaneous the way guilt filled me. I wasn't doing anything wrong, at least not morally so, but I had been keeping Easton from Theo.

And that felt like one of the worst things I could do.

"Hey, Theo." I wiped my mouth with my napkin and sat up straighter in my booth. "What are you doing here?"

He pointed to a table toward the front of the restaurant. "Me and some of the guys just came to eat after practice."

"Cool." I nodded, and I knew that I looked like a lunatic.

"Easton." Theo gave him a chin lift, but it didn't seem friendly even if they were in the same fraternity. "Can I borrow Maddison for a second? I just want to talk to her about our weekend plans."

We didn't have any weekend plans, but I didn't think the actuality of Theo's reasoning mattered to him or Easton. I caught the small tick in Easton's jaw before he smiled over at me.

"Of course. I promise I won't eat all the egg rolls while you're gone." The wink he shot in my direction was in the perfect view for Theo to see.

I slid out of the booth with a tight smile on my face and followed Theo toward the register. I knew he was going to question me about why I was with Easton, but I wasn't prepared for the way he turned in my direction with anger on his face.

"What are you doing?" His question was as short as his voice, and I could feel my pulse in my neck.

"I'm eating lunch." I ran my sweaty hands down my jeans.

"I can see that." He huffed. "But what are you doing with Easton Cole?" He pointed back to where Easton was sitting waiting on me, and I looked back to make sure he was still there.

"He's my group project partner in English." I told the half-truth. "I didn't know it was an issue."

"He's too old for you." He lowered his voice for only me to hear.

My brow tensed in frustration. "He's not that much older than me."

"He is." He stepped closer to me. "And far more experienced. I don't want anyone taking advantage of you. I don't care if he is my frat brother."

I wanted to tell him that he didn't know anything. That he didn't know what my experience consisted of, but the truth was that he did. Theo and I had never kept things from each other.

Not until now.

"He's not taking advantage of me, Theo. We're having lunch not an orgy. He's my TA. My professor assigned us as partners, he didn't pick me out of the lot."

He frowned, his eyes creeping back to where Easton sat, but I brought his attention back to me when I placed my hand over his.

"I don't like him." The words were passed his lips before I could say anything.

"Since when?" I laughed. "You never told me that you had problems with him before."

"Well, I'm telling you now." He looked dead serious, as if he couldn't see how ridiculous he was being.

"Okay, Theo." I patted his chest. "I think I can handle myself."

I turned in the direction of Easton, but Theo grabbed my hand to stop me. "Just be careful. Okay?"

"Always."

He nodded his head but didn't look convinced.

"I'll call you later. Okay?"

"Yeah." He dropped my hand. "I'll see you later."

CHAPTER 14

I DIDN'T KNOW where we were going, but Easton told me to bring a sweater and an overnight bag.

I lied to Theo when he asked me if I wanted to go to one of their parties with him. I told him that I had too much studying to do, and I was going to stay in. I felt like trash as the lie left my lips, but I knew he would never understand. He would die if he knew what I was doing now. That I was in a truck with Easton while he drove us to a place that I had no clue where.

He would call me stupid and reckless, and maybe I was, but I couldn't stop the butterflies in my stomach as I looked over at Easton with one hand on the steering wheel and the other linked with mine.

We had only been driving for a little over an hour when Easton pulled the truck into a hotel parking lot.

"This is where you're taking me?" I arched an eyebrow at him, and he laughed.

We were on the outskirts of Atlanta. I knew because I had been to Atlanta plenty of times with my parents.

"No. This isn't where I'm taking you. I just want to check us in real quick before it gets too late."

I followed him into the hotel as he carried both of our bags, and I stood beside him as he checked us in. He gripped my hand in his and led me to the room before setting our bags on the bed.

"We need to get ready." He opened the curtains on the far wall. "The sun is starting to set."

"What exactly are we going to do?" I sat down on the edge of the bed. "Are we burying a body? Is that what was in the back of the truck?"

"Not quite." He laughed as he leaned down and pressed his hands against the mattress on either side of me. "But you've trusted me this far. Now throw on some comfy pants and a sweatshirt."

He pressed a chaste kiss to my lips before pulling away and rummaging through his own bag.

I did as he said. I grabbed my yoga pants out of my bag along with a t-shirt and sweatshirt, and I closed the door to the bathroom as I began getting dressed. Once I was ready, for what I didn't know, I walked out of the bathroom to find Easton wearing a pair of sweatpants and a t-shirt.

I had no earthly clue where he was taking me or what we were doing.

But for some odd reason, I trusted him, and I never trusted anyone so explicitly except for Theo.

We climbed back in his truck, and I rested my head against the headrest and watched him as he drove. He was excited, his smile never leaving his face, and I couldn't help but feel that same giddy feeling.

When I saw the sign, I could barely catch my breath. I leaned forward trying to get a better look, and Easton was watching me.

"Is this where we're going?" I asked, my voice filled with excitement as we got closer and closer to the Starlight Drive-In Theater sign.

"We are." He turned on to the gravel road leading us to the small stand to pay for our tickets, and I couldn't stop smiling as I bounced in my seat.

Easton purchased our tickets before pulling forward and parking the truck in the middle of the lot. I looked out his rear window at the huge screen, and I jumped out of the truck before Easton could make it to my side. There were families all around, parking their cars, pulling out chairs, and some kids throwing a football.

Easton pulled the large tarp off the bed of his truck, and I had never been so excited in my life to see a pallet of blankets and pillows.

"This might be the best day of my life."

Easton laughed at my dramatics, but I wasn't kidding. I had dreamed of going to a drive-in movie ever since I first saw *Grease* when I was eight years old. There was something about it that just seemed so dreamy and nostalgic, and I couldn't believe that I was actually here.

Easton pulled out a radio and adjusted it to the station on the paper they had given us when we bought our tickets. Fifties music began playing through the speakers, and I could hear the echo of the song playing throughout every car at the drive-in.

"Are you hungry?" Easton nodded toward the small concession stand that was toward the back of the theater.

"Of course, I am." I grabbed his hand in mine, and the two of us bobbed and weaved through cars and playing kids as we made our way to the concession stand.

As soon as the door opened, the smell hit me. It reminded me of a carnival—fried food, sugar confections, and everything good in this world that we're told we're not supposed to have. Easton ordered a burger and fries while I ordered a footlong corn dog and onion rings. He pulled a huge bag of pink cotton candy down from a hook and tucked it under his arm as we made our way to the register, and in that moment, I didn't know what I had done in my life to deserve a guy like him.

It didn't matter that we weren't official or that we couldn't be. All that mattered was that he was here with me when he could have chosen to be anywhere else.

We carried our food to the truck and Easton's hands gripped my hips as he lifted me into the truck bed. The sun was sinking below the large theater screen and the sky was bathed in swirling colors of pink and orange.

I quickly grabbed my camera out of my bag and snapped a shot of the sky before catching Easton completely off guard and snapping one of him eating. He finally noticed my camera and crossed his eyes as a drop of ketchup fell down his bottom lip, and I saved that moment forever with the click of my lens.

I set my camera near my feet and picked up my corn dog to start eating. "You didn't have to do all this." I waved my corn dog around, meaning everything that he had done for me. The camera, the theater, all of it.

"I wanted to." He popped another fry in his mouth and his blue eyes were smiling at me.

"You know, when I first saw you, this is not the guy I expected you to be."

He chuckled around his food before swallowing. "Who did you think I'd be?"

"I don't know. More dangerous. A heartbreaker. A bad boy."

His grin took over his face as he leaned back against the pillow, and I almost choked on my corn dog. He was so handsome, so effortlessly breathtaking, and I couldn't look at him without feeling a tightness in my chest that I hadn't felt before.

"I'm a total bad boy." He lifted his arm behind his head.

"I don't think so." I shook my head. "I've never seen a bad boy carrying around such a big bag of cotton candy."

He pulled a piece of cotton candy out of the bag and pressed it to his tongue. The music had stopped on the radio, and they were now talking about the start of the movie since the sun had all but disappeared and left darkness behind. But I didn't care.

The only thing I could focus on was that small flash of pink I saw on his tongue and the way he moaned at the sweet taste.

"Here's the thing about cotton candy." He leaned toward me and held a small piece out to me. I instantly opened my mouth, and he ran the fluffy candy along my lips as he spoke. "All it needs is your tongue." He pressed the candy to my tongue before pulling it away again. I could see the way it was already melting from his tongue as he traced it against my neck. The sticky candy stuck to my skin as he trailed it down and over my collarbone, and I held my breath as his head lowered to the same path. "It's so sweet," he murmured against my skin. "And so wet."

His tongue pressed against my skin, licking away every trace of sugar that he left there, and I could feel my pulse between my thighs. It seemed to beat harder and harder with every swipe of his tongue, and I didn't care that we were in the middle of a drive-in theater. I didn't care that the movie was starting, and I was missing it. The only thing that mattered was how badly I wanted him.

I pushed against him, his back hitting the pillows once again, and I straddled his lap as I leaned down against him. No one could see us in the back of his truck, not unless they were standing directly beside it, but there was still a thrill that ran through me at the thought of being caught with him.

He was too eager to wait for me. He leaned up, pressing his lips to mine, before he buried his hand in my hair and brought me down with him. His kiss was erotic, his tongue fighting with mine, his teeth swelling my lips, and I breathed him in over and over so I wouldn't miss a single second of it.

I rocked my hips against his, and he groaned, deep and low. The sound had a direct line to my pussy, and I found myself trying to tighten my thighs around him. Easton pushed me off him, rolling me to my back, before following my body. He was half pressed against mine, half on the truck, but he never stopped kissing me.

His hand found the skin of my side where my sweatshirt had lifted, and he rested it there, his fingers digging into my skin as if that was the one thing holding every bit of his control. But I didn't want his control. I wanted his chaos. I wanted him wild.

I gripped his hand in mine and moved it down, over my yoga pants, and he didn't hesitate as he cupped my sex. His hand was rough, the pressure shooting straight through my stomach, and I rocked against his hand, begging him for more.

Easton moved then, his body leaving mine as he moved toward the end of the tailgate, and I was so disappointed, so fucking turned on, that I couldn't stop my small whimper of frustration.

But he wasn't done with me. He tugged my feet toward him, lowering me onto the pillows a little bit more, and he lifted a blanket over his back before he laid his body beside my legs.

I squirmed, trying to open them for him, trying to give him as much access as he wanted, but he squeezed my thighs together and held them there as his teeth nipped at the sliver of skin exposed at my stomach.

I took a rushed breath as he quickly pulled my pants and panties down my hips. He left them resting there, barely exposing the top of my pussy, but I could feel the night air against me. I looked up at the stars as I waited for his next move with bated breath. His lips pressed against the top of me, a gentle, slow kiss, and I squirmed again under his touch.

He continued peppering those small, almost innocent kisses then his tongue caught me off guard as it slid through the top of my slit and pressed against my clit.

I covered my mouth with my hand to try to muffle my moans, but it was almost impossible. Everything Easton had just been doing, the soft kisses, the good boy act, it was gone, and in its place was everything I had thought about him when I first laid eyes on him.

His hand reached out and I watched him grab another piece of cotton candy. The blanket had fallen to his shoulders, and he didn't seem to care. He didn't care that there were at least a hundred other people beside us silently watching the movie. He laid the cotton candy against my sex and slowly ran his tongue against it. I watched him, his eyes on me, as he dissolved the candy against me, making my breathing turn ragged. Then he sucked my clit between his lips and my back arched against the truck bed as I whispered his name. We were going to get caught. Not in the same way that had thrilled me moments before. Now we were going to get caught with his hand buried between my legs and my body shaking beneath him. We were going to get caught while I begged him to never stop.

Easton's hands forced my legs tighter together, and I had never experienced anything like it—the pressure of my own legs, his tongue being forced between them. It was overwhelming and delicious, and I couldn't figure out what it was I wanted. My legs shook and tried to open on their own accord so he could have full access, but silently I begged him not to let them. There was something about him being in control, of him taking my pleasure from me in the way that he saw fit, that made me wetter than I had ever been before.

He buried his mouth against me, his teeth grazing gently over my clit, and I buried my head into the pillow next to me as I screamed through the hardest orgasm of my life.

I didn't know what was happening as the last shockwave ran through my body and Easton laid back beside me again. He was smiling, a wicked smile that did nothing to help bring me down from my orgasm, and he ran his finger over the edge of my pussy before he helped me pull my pants back where they belonged.

I reached out, trying to touch him, but he stopped me.

"Watch the movie, Maddison. This is your bucket list item." He slid his arm underneath my head and pulled me closer to him.

"But I have other bucket list items too." I licked my lips, and he watched.

"Then who am I to deny you?" He grinned, and I don't know what I was thinking calling him anything other than dangerous.

Because that's exactly what he was.

But I didn't seem to care as I lowered myself down his body and missed every bit of the movie.

CHAPTER 15

I REMEMBER WAKING up as Easton carried me to the cab of the truck, but it didn't last long. As soon as he laid me down there, I was back asleep as if the whole thing was just a dream.

I didn't fully wake up until the engine died and I looked up to see we were back at the hotel. It was way beyond midnight, the second movie had lulled me to sleep, and I rubbed the sleep out of my eyes as Easton moved around the truck and opened the door for me.

He reached inside like he was going to carry me all the way to our room, but I pushed his hand away with a chuckle.

"I can walk, you know." I stretched my arms over my head and his eyes instantly went to my breast.

"That wouldn't be very chivalrous of me though, would it."

"I'm sure you'll be fine." I patted his chest and climbed out of the truck. "I'm not looking for a Prince Charming."

"Or maybe you're looking for the wrong one." He pushed his black hair out of his face as he grinned at me.

"Maybe." I closed the door behind me, and he laced his fingers with mine as we walked side by side to our room.

His hair was disheveled, probably due to a combination of his hands and mine, and he had a sleepy smile on his face as he pushed the key into the door. I couldn't wait for the door to open. I couldn't wait until we were lying in the same bed staring at each other with secret smiles. I needed him. More than I ever needed anything before.

I pressed my body against his as he turned the handle, and his hands gripped my ass just as I slammed my mouth to his. He lifted me in the air, my thighs wrapping around him instantly, and I could feel how badly he wanted me between my thighs.

We hit the wall, the inside of the hotel room pitch black, and I laughed as Easton almost tripped over something on the floor. My laughter died as he grazed his teeth against my neck, and I tightened my thighs around him, trying like hell to pull him even closer.

We fell to the bed, my back hitting the mattress before his body weight came down on me, and I moaned as my thighs opened and I finally felt him exactly where I needed him.

"Fuck, Maddison." Easton ripped his t-shirt from his back, and I reached down, pulling his sweatpants to his knees before finishing the job with my feet.

He was completely naked. Completely bare in front of me, and my hands shook as I pulled my own shirt over my head. He was so beautiful, heartbreakingly so, and I suddenly felt self-conscious.

But he didn't let it last. He slowly pulled my pants and panties down my legs as he stared at me. "You are so beautiful."

I listened to his words, and I let them run through me. There was nothing left between us as I unsnapped my bra.

No rules, no Theo, no reasons we shouldn't be together.

It was just me and him.

He leaned forward, gripping my head in his hand, and he kissed me like he felt it too.

His body pressed against mine, and I rolled against him trying to feel more of him. His mouth left mine, running over my jaw, tracing a path down my neck, and I spread my thighs, forcing him closer.

"We don't have to do this," he whispered against my collarbone. "We don't need to have sex."

I didn't have a single speck of doubt that I wanted him, that I wanted this, but there was something about knowing this wasn't all he wanted me for that seemed to make me want him more.

"Please don't stop," I begged as I clung to his shoulders.

He looked up at me, his blue eyes searching my brown ones. "Are you sure?"

"Yes." I nodded my head. I had never been more sure about anything in my life. "Please."

His leg touched my inner thigh, and I shivered in anticipation. He gripped his cock in his hand, and I felt him against me. He rubbed himself along my slit and he groaned when he felt how wet I was for him.

He teased me, rubbing up and down against my clit, and I cried out at the sensation. He lined himself up with me, and I tensed as he pushed into me. I felt impossibly full as he pushed in and out, and I was embarrassingly close to orgasm just from a simple grind of his hips.

"Easton," I called his name just as his thumb started rubbing small circles against my clit.

"I know." He moaned against me. "I know, baby."

I fell apart around him then. My thighs tightened so hard around him I didn't know how he still managed to move, but he did. He milked every ounce of my orgasm out of me before he followed me over the edge.

His chest was heaving against mine as we both tried to catch our breaths. Easton may not have been my Prince Charming, but he was everything I needed. At least for now. At least until the rest of the world told me he wasn't.

He lifted his face from my neck, and his eyes were a softer shade of blue than I had ever seen them. He looked happy, deliriously so, and I knew that I would chase the high of putting that look on his face for as long as he'd let me.

"Go to the homecoming formal with me." His words were a whisper but then slammed into me like a ton of bricks.

"What?" My body became tense beneath him, and I knew that he could feel it.

"The homecoming formal. I know it's a bit lame, but I want to take you."

I knew that I should have said yes. I wanted to say yes, but I had already agreed to go with Theo, and I hated the idea of letting either one of them down.

"I can't." I shook my head.

"Don't worry about my position." He pushed a stray piece of hair out of my face. "The professors won't be there, and honestly, I don't care."

"It's not that." My chest felt heavy, like someone was pushing against my breastbone, and I hated saying the next words that passed my lips. "I already told Theo I'd go with him."

His face fell even though he tried to hide it with a smile, and for the first time since Theo asked me, I wished I hadn't said yes.

"Our parents are coming in for the homecoming game. He asked me before school even started," I rushed to explain.

"It's okay, Maddison." His fingers cupped the back of my neck, and he gently lifted my face to meet his. His lips were a whisper over mine before he spoke. "Just promise to save a dance for me."

"Promise." My answer was immediate, and Easton chuckled before pressing his lips back against mine.

CHAPTER 16

I HAD NEVER BEEN SO nervous about a formal in my entire life.

Dillon curled my hair before pulling it all back out of my face in an updo that I would have never been able to accomplish on my own. My makeup was heavier than I normally wore, the deep smoky eye bringing out my eyes, and somehow the nude lipstick seemed to do the same with my lips.

Dillon helped me zip my deep royal blue dress that was tight in the bodice before the silk cascaded to the ground. My shoulders were completely bare with no straps or jewelry. Only a pair of small diamonds that Theo had given me for my high school graduation dangled from my ears.

Dillon was wearing a hot pink dress that fit her body like a second skin, and she looked amazing. Her blonde hair stood out against her tan skin, and I couldn't wait to see what her date thought of her.

I hadn't met him, but she had met him at one of the fraternity parties. She went way more than I did.

Dillon and I laughed as we walked down the steps to the front door of our dorm, and even though I wasn't exactly looking forward to this, Dillon's excitement was enough for the both of us.

Theo and Dillon's date were both outside the door as we pushed outside the door, but I could only look at Theo. His hair was pushed back and styled and looked perfect against the black of his suit. His white shirt beneath was a crisp white and a classic black tie hung down his chest.

He looked the best I had ever seen him, and it was impossible for my stomach not to flutter when he looked up at me.

"Maddy," he said my name as his eyes roamed over my dress in awe. I could see him taking in the smallest details—the curve of my hip below the thin fabric, the swell of my breasts that peeked out of the sweetheart neckline. "You look gorgeous."

He wrapped his arm around my waist, and I smiled up at my best friend. It felt weird that now that I was here, now that I was at the same college, it was the farthest I had ever felt from him. Even when we were a hundred miles apart, I talked to him every day. I felt like I knew everything about him.

But I was wrong.

And I missed him.

"Thank you." I ran my finger over his tie. "You're looking pretty handsome yourself."

He smiled and took my hand in his as he led us toward his car. Dillon and her date climbed in the backseat as Theo held the front door open for me.

When we pulled up to the auditorium where the formal was being held, I was surprised by the number of cars that filled the parking lot. We had to drive around twice to find a spot, and I was cursing my choice of heels when I saw how far we had to walk.

Theo made sure to open my door again, and he wrapped my arm around his as we walked toward the auditorium.

"I can give you a piggyback ride." He looked down at my heels with a smile.

"Do you know how high I would have to hike this dress?" I wagged my eyebrows. "We would be giving the entire campus a show."

His brown eyes seemed to turn to fire. "We don't want to do that."

"No," I agreed with him. "We don't."

The auditorium was decorated elegantly with black and gold and touches of red for school spirit. Theo was instantly bombarded as we walked through the door. Everyone wanting to talk about the game tomorrow night and their predictions of the score.

Theo entertained them all, but he never once let go of my arm as I stood next to him. He would look down at me every few seconds, and I knew that if I told him to, he would have walked away from everyone else completely.

"You want to dance?" Theo nodded toward the dance floor as one guy continued to ramble on about offense and defense and our opponent's lack of one or the other.

"Yeah." I grinned and tightened my hand around his bicep.

"Jake." He patted the guy on the shoulder mid-sentence. "We'll be back. My girl here wants to dance, and I need to show her off in this fine ass dress."

I scoffed at his words and the way Jake seemed to notice I was standing there for the first time all night, but Theo was already pulling me in the direction of the dance floor. He swirled me, the tail of my skirt fluttering with the movement, and I laughed as I wrapped my arms around his shoulders.

"You really do look beautiful tonight." He moved me slowly to the music, matching the dance of everyone around us, and I knew that my chest was turning red under his praise.

"Thank you, Theo." My fingers toyed with the collar of his suit. "They were all sold out of the puffy dresses I knew you were looking forward to."

He laughed, the sound as smooth as butter. "It's a shame, really." His hand flexed against my back. "Now all of these guys get to see how hot you really are."

"You saying I wouldn't have been hot with the layers of tulle?"

"You'd be hot in anything." He twirled me around again, and I watched the world spin around us in a swirl of lights and strangers.

We danced until my feet hurt and I was dying of thirst. I

sat down at a table with a group of people I only recognized from his parties, and Theo kissed the top of my head before he moved toward the refreshment table to grab us some drinks.

"So," the girl to my left said as she leaned toward me. "Are you and Theo dating?"

"No." I shook my head. "We're just friends."

I hated the way her eyes lit up at my words regardless of the date who sat at her side oblivious to our conversation.

"That's good to know." She looked across the table to one of her friends. "I was disappointed when he didn't ask me to the formal, but it's good to know it was a pity date."

I shifted backward as if she had slapped me. "It's not a pity date. He asked me before school even started."

"Oh. I didn't mean it like that." She smiled the fakest smile I had ever seen. "I just meant that it's nice to know that he decided to still go with you out of pity when he's been sleeping with me."

Jealousy ran wild through every inch of me.

Theo wasn't mine, but it didn't matter.

It didn't matter that I didn't want to be his anymore.

I didn't want him to be hers either.

Theo returned to the table before either of us could say more, and my back straightened as he set my punch in front of me and took the seat between us.

He started talking to one of the guys at our table, not noticing the tense air at our table, and I listened to him talk for a few minutes before I stood from my seat.

"Where are you going?" Theo smiled at me over his shoulder, and that simple look reminded me so much of the Theo I grew up with, the Theo I loved, and I knew that I couldn't be mad at him when he'd been nothing short of an amazing best friend.

"I'm just going to the bathroom." I hiked my finger over my shoulder, pointing in that direction.

"Okay." He turned back toward his friends without noticing an ounce of my unease, and I ran my hands down my dress to straighten the fabric before I made my way to escape.

I was almost to the door, almost to the place where I could take deep breaths without anyone noticing, when a hand firmly gripped my bicep and stopped my advance.

"Fuck, Maddison." I looked up at the sound of Easton's voice, and I almost fell to my knees by the way he was looking at me. "You look so damn gorgeous."

He said almost the same words that Theo had said earlier, but it didn't feel the same.

Theo's words didn't make me feel like I was the only girl he could see.

But Easton's did.

"Thank you." I was breathless as I stared at him. He was wearing a black suit similar to Theo's, but he wore a simple black shirt beneath with the top button unbuttoned. His hair was pushed back out of his face in tantalizing perfection and my hands ached with the urge to run them through it.

He looked dark and off limits.

Completely untouchable.

And I wanted him more than I had ever wanted anything else before.

"You look incredible."

He smiled at my compliment and pressed his finger just below my chin to force me to look up at him.

"I wish you had come with me." His warm breath caressed my lips, and I felt trapped in everything he was. Everything around us faded away, and I started to forget that we weren't supposed to be together. That people weren't supposed to know that we were more than what we seemed.

"Do you want to dance?" His voice was like a drug, and I couldn't stop myself from leaning in and begging for more.

"Yes." I nodded my head against his finger that still held my face captive.

He smiled, a full devastating smile, before he linked his fingers with mine and led me to the dance floor. No one looked at us as we passed, but my skin felt like pins and needles. There was an electricity around us, a rush about being with him when everyone could see us.

His fingers tightened around mine as he pulled me toward him, my body pressing against every inch of his, and he lifted my hands to his shoulders before he let his fall away.

His hand slid around my back and rested at the small ridge just above my ass and the other took a slower route—a slow caress down my arm. He traced every curve and angle before his hand finally reached my hip, and I couldn't do anything except concentrate on breathing and not falling into everything that he was.

He leaned down and his voice was a whisper by my ear. "I missed you." His lips pressed against my cheek before he slowly pulled away.

I told my heart to calm down. We had just seen each other last night. We had spent so much time together that we should be tired of each other, but my heart wasn't listening. I was already missing him too, and it felt absurd the way I seemed to breathe easier when he was around.

"I missed you too."

The scent of his cologne was addictive, and I found myself pushing closer to him when already there wasn't an inch of space.

There were couples spinning around us on the dance floor, but I wouldn't be able to recall any of their faces come morning. I was too busy staring at Easton, at the way his bowed lips silently mouthed the words to the song and the way he couldn't seem to take his eyes off me.

His fingers flexed against my back, my dress bunching under his touch, and my core tightened as those same fingers trembled as he tried to relax them again.

"Can I cut in?"

Easton's body went stiff against mine as we both looked over at Theo, but I forced a smile on my face.

"Of course." I let my hands fall from Easton's shoulders, but his didn't budge from me. Instead, they tightened, and I feared he was going to tell Theo. He was going to risk everything to tell the boy I had loved almost half my life that I was now falling in love with someone else.

Theo was staring at Easton's hand on my hip and the skin underneath began to burn. I didn't know if it was the way Easton's fingers pressed into my skin or the way Theo's eyes blazed in anger or the combination of the two. Either way, I knew I wouldn't survive between them.

I gently pushed against Easton's chest and his attention snapped back to me. I silently begged him to let it go, to remember why he told me we couldn't be together in this way, and although his own burning gaze didn't cool in the slightest, he finally released his hold on me.

"Save another dance for me." He winked at me with a heartbreaking smirk on his face directly where Theo could see, and I couldn't help smiling. Even if it was idiotic and childish, Easton laying any sort of claim over me where Theo could see turned me on.

Easton moved back toward the outskirts of the makeshift ballroom, and Theo didn't hesitate as he pulled me into him and started moving me around the floor. His body was much stiffer against mine than before, almost robotic, and I followed his gaze that seemed to be glued to Easton's every move.

"Are you okay?" I asked as I turned us, forcing him to turn his attention to me.

"I'm fine." His answer was clipped and gruff, and even though I knew it wouldn't make the situation any better, I chuckled at his answer.

His brow scrunched in frustration as he stared at me. He wasn't happy. Not with me dancing with Easton and not with me laughing at his irritation.

"Are you seriously mad that I was dancing with someone else?" I rolled my eyes good-naturedly and tightened my hand around my neck. "I didn't realize this formal was an exclusive thing."

He didn't laugh at my joke. Instead, he looked over his shoulder before looking back at me. "Why him? I told you that I didn't like him."

"What exactly don't you like about him?" I asked, but he didn't answer. "He's my friend, Theo. I'm allowed to have other friends."

He shook his head in exasperation. "He doesn't want to be your friend."

His words ran through me like a hot iron. "Neither does your buddy over at your table." I nodded in the direction of the girl who pissed me off earlier.

His brow scrunched in confusion. "What does Emmy have to do with this?"

Emmy. I hated her name as much as I hated her.

"Well, according to Emmy, I'm just a pity date since you've been fucking her and plan on fucking her once you leave here."

He looked shocked. From what I had said or the fact that I had actually called him on something, I wasn't sure, but it took him a moment to compose himself before he managed to say anything back to me. "You are not a pity date."

Every single word was clear. Every single one honest, but I didn't care.

"But you are planning to fuck her after you drop me off at my dorm, right?" I turned my head to the side and watched him as his strong, square jaw shifted.

"Is that really something we want to discuss?" He ran his fingers through his hair, and I was glad that it messed it up some. He looked too perfect before, too fake.

"I don't know, Theo." We were still dancing, still moving around the room as if we weren't having the first real fight of our entire friendship. "You want to talk about how you would feel if I fucked Easton."

His hands around me tightened, and they felt so wrong compared to Easton's.

And more than anything, I hated that I felt that way.

I hated that he was going to fuck her even though I couldn't stop thinking about Easton. It was fucked up. We were a spinning pair of hypocrites on the dance floor, but I didn't care. I needed to know what he was thinking. I was dying to know.

"You're not going to fuck Easton." His face moved minutely closer to mine. "He's not good enough for you, he's too old for you, and I'm not going to let him take advantage of you."

"For God's sake, what do you think is going to happen? Do you think he's going to lure me into his dungeon and never let me out? You live in the same house for crying out loud."

He didn't listen to a word I said because he didn't care.

"He's your TA, Maddison." He called me my full first name for the first time in so long that I forgot what it sounded like coming from his mouth. "He's not allowed to be with you."

"Don't you want me to be happy?" I whispered the words I was afraid to ask. I was worried that Theo just wanted us to stay the same. But I couldn't be the girl who was there for him through everything when he wasn't willing to do the same for me.

"Of course, I do." He pulled me tighter against him still. "But not with him."

I planted my feet into the floor and stopped our dance in its tracks. "What do you want from me?"

"Nothing," he said the word I had been dreading for half my life, but the burn wasn't as nearly as strong as I had expected. "I just need to protect you."

His fingers reached out and touched my earlobe, the earring he bought me feeling like a brand in his hands. "We've been protecting each other for almost half our lives."

"I don't need you to protect me anymore." I shook my head.

"You do." He looked over my shoulder before he gently turned my face in the same direction. Easton was leaning against the wall toward the back of the room and beside him stood a tall, gorgeous girl who looked like everything I wasn't. She was older than me and far more composed, and I wanted to rip every piece of hair out of her head as she laughed at something Easton was saying. "Easton's a player, Maddy. I live with the guy. You don't think I've seen what he does to girls? That I haven't had to listen to them cry when he breaks their hearts? I won't let him do that to you."

I didn't know what to believe. I didn't think Easton was capable of the things Theo was saying, but Theo had never lied to me before. He had no reason to lie to me, and I was a fucking fool.

I watched as the girl laid her hand on Easton's arm, and I silently begged him to push her away. Or to look at me. One simple look and I wouldn't have given two shits what Theo was saying to me, but he didn't do either. Instead, he turned closer to her as they spoke, and I took a deep breath to steady myself and my crumbling, stupid heart.

CHAPTER 17

I WENT BACK to the frat house with Theo like a complete idiot. There was a party happening of course, which I had no interest in, but I wanted to see Easton's face when he walked in the door. I wanted to confront him. I wanted to make him feel as small as I did now.

Easton: Where are you?

I read his text message over and over before I finally replied.

I'm with Theo.

His next message was immediate and playful, and I wanted to smack him through my phone.

Easton: I wanted to dance with you again. I can't get how you looked out of my head. Can I see you tonight?

Even though those simple words made me crave what he said, I knew that falling for Easton Cole was the worst possible idea I had ever come up with. Because he had the power to break me, and I wasn't in the mood to be broken.

I'm staying with Theo.

I looked up from my phone as Theo laughed at something someone said, but my phone buzzed in my hand within seconds.

Easton: What happened?

I hated that he already knew me so well, that he could pick up that something was wrong with me over the phone when Theo hadn't been able to sitting right beside me.

Theo told me.

About what you do. About how you play girls. I can't believe you.

I wasn't in the mood to fuck around. I wanted him to know that I knew. I wanted him to feel exactly like I felt even though I knew he wouldn't.

Because Theo told me in the car ride back to the dorm that I was just another girl to Easton. It was why he had originally warned me away from him. It was why he didn't want me near him.

Easton: What are you talking about?

Easton: Where are you?

Easton: I need to see you.

His text messages came one after another in a rapid succession, and I hated that my heart ached at his words.

Find another girl, Easton. I'm staying with Theo.

Theo nudged my shoulder and I forced a smile as I looked up at him. We were both still in our dressy outfits from the formal, everyone at the party was, and the dress suddenly felt wrong against my skin. When I had bought it, I was thinking about Easton. I was trying to imagine what his reaction would be when he saw me, when his hands touched the silky fabric, but now I hated that I had bought this dress for him.

Easton: Theo is a joke. He just wants to keep you in the friend zone where he can lead you on for as long as he can.

I struggled to inhale as I read his words.

Fuck you.

My phone buzzed in my hand again, but I turned it off before I could read it. I didn't care what else Easton had to say. He had already hurt me enough, and I wasn't going to be his punching bag. I grabbed a cup from the table in front of me along with a brown bottle of liquor and I poured myself three fingers of whiskey before I set the bottle back on the table. Theo was watching me like he wanted to say something, like he wanted to stop me, but I didn't care.

He was just as bad as Easton.

Neither of them cared about me—not in the way that I cared about them, and I was tired of listening to stupid boys telling me what I should do.

"I'm going to grab you a Coke to go with that," Theo said as he stood, but I lifted it to my mouth and let the whiskey burn my throat as I emptied the cup.

Theo set the soda down in front of me, as I started pouring more liquor, and I dared him with my eyes to say something to me. I was raring for a fight. I was begging for it, but he simply took his seat next to me and watched as I threw back more whiskey than I had ever had in my life.

I watched the people around me. The happy couples. The flirting. The guys obsessively talking about football.

These people felt like gods of this school, and I guess they were. But in reality, none of this mattered. I knew that. I knew how trivial all of this seemed, but I still couldn't seem to bury that sinking feeling in my stomach with enough whiskey.

My nose was tingling by the time I finally saw Easton walk through the door. He was alone, the girl from the formal nowhere in sight, and his gaze was laser-focused on me.

I couldn't tell if he was upset or angry as I lifted the whiskey to my lips again, but I knew with one hundred percent certainty that I didn't want to care.

He took a step toward me, and I turned away from him and searched out Theo at my side. Even if I felt pissed at him too, he was safe. He had been my safety for as long as I could remember.

And even though I didn't know this Theo like my Theo, I knew that he had never let me down before.

He wrapped his arm around my waist as I pressed against his side, and I tried my best not to look over at Easton as he stood across from us. He started talking with some of the guys around him, his gaze moving to me every few seconds, and I felt unsteady on my feet. Whether it was from him or the whiskey, I wasn't sure.

Theo's hand tightened around my waist when he noticed him, and I was thankful for the support.

"Theo." Easton smiled in Theo's direction. "Where's your girl at tonight? That one you've been keeping us all awake with lately."

All the guys around the group laughed, and I physically recoiled in Theo's touch. But he held firm.

"I'm sure she's around here somewhere," Theo said without hesitation before cocking his head to the side with a smirk on his face. "Where's yours?"

The people around us seemed to notice the tension for the first time because the conversations around us came to a stop and everyone was looking between Theo and Easton.

"I don't have one anymore." His eyes finally aimed in my direction, if only for a second, and I felt like I couldn't breathe. "You think you can loan me one of yours for the night?"

I hated his words. I hated how everyone chuckled again like it was the funniest thing in the world to discuss sharing women.

"I'm sure you can find someone around here." Theo chuckled. "But I'm not into sharing." He pulled me farther into his side. "You'll have to find someone who isn't already mine."

I didn't look up at Easton to see his reaction. Instead, I stared at the bottle of whiskey I left on the table and prayed that the large amount that I had already drunk would make me forget this night all together. With every breath that I inhaled, I could feel the pain taking over my chest. It crept through my body, like oxygen in my blood, and I knew everyone could see it. My heartbreak felt as much a part of me as anything else.

But then Easton laughed, a laugh that was filled with

anything but joy, and he grabbed the hand of a blonde who stood right behind him before whispering in her ear. She laughed at whatever he said, and I hated him in that moment. He pointed down at her as he stared at Theo. "This one okay?"

Everyone laughed again including Theo as Easton walked off hand in hand with the girl, and I could feel the whiskey and lack of food in my stomach crawling up my throat.

I didn't realize the power Easton had over me until that moment. He was destroying me, not just the version of me that I was when I met him, but that ounce of braveness that he had instilled in me to be who I truly was, I could feel it crumbling.

I pushed away from Theo as soon as Easton rounded the stairs, and I pressed my hand against my stomach.

I was just tipsy enough to do something stupid, and I was pissed enough not to care.

I moved toward the stairs when Theo grabbed my hand in his and stopped me.

"Don't." There was so much judgment in his eyes as he shook his head.

I jerked my hand out of his without a word, and I climbed up the stairs that Easton had just taken moments before. His door was closed when I got upstairs, but I didn't care. I turned the handle without pause, and I was surprised when it opened.

Easton was sitting on his bed, his hands behind him holding him up, and the girl was standing in front of him. He looked up at me as I closed the door behind me, and I hated the empty look in his eyes. This wasn't the Easton I was falling for, this was someone else, and I knew that I didn't like him.

"What are you doing here, Maddison?" He looked bored as he spoke to me. "Me and..." He hesitated as he looked up at her.

"Jemma."

"Jemma and I were just about to have some fun. Unless you're here to join us." He smirked at me, his words hitting their mark. "That is what you told me, right? That's what I do to girls."

I knew he was teasing me, that he wanted me to hurt, but I wasn't willing to give myself over to him that easily. I walked toward him, and even though he was being cruel, his gaze still ran over my body as if no one else was in the room. He wasn't even looking at Jemma, but he was about to.

I stepped up behind her and pressed my breasts against her back as I looked at Easton over her shoulder. I didn't drop his stare as I lowered my head and pressed my lips against her shoulder.

"Maddison," he whispered my name, and I only let it fuel me.

I reached in front of Jemma and gently gripped her chin in my hand as I turned her face toward me. Her eyes were glazed over in lust, but I still silently asked her permission with mine. She nodded her head in my hand, just barely, and I licked my lips before pressing them to hers.

She wasn't hesitant. Her lips opened as she slid her tongue against mine and her hand reached up and gripped my arm just below my elbow.

Kissing her was so different from kissing him. She was softer, her skin velvety against mine, and the smell of her perfume overwhelmed me.

I pulled away from her lips and drew a path with my lips to her neck. Her body shuddered beneath my touch, and I met Easton's gaze as I ran my tongue just below her earlobe to drive her wild like he had once done to me.

She moaned, the softest little whimper, and I could see the proof of Easton's arousal in the front of his pants. She reached behind her, searching for me, and I let her touch me as Easton watched. Her dress fell from her body with one simple zip, and

Easton watched the fabric fall to the floor before looking back up at me.

My fingers grazed the swell of her breasts before pressing against her stomach. She took a deep breath before she turned to me and helped me out of my own dress. Her hand trailed down my spine as the fabric fell away and chill bumps broke out along my body. Easton sat up fully in the bed and pulled off his black jacket.

Jemma was rushed as her hands moved around my body, and I was shocked when she dipped her fingers below my black lace panties and pressed against my core. Easton was on me then. His lips touched mine as Jemma's fingers began creating small circles against my clit, and he swallowed my whimpers of pleasure.

I felt overstimulated with him in front of me and her behind, but I didn't want any of it to stop. Instead, I wrapped my arms around Easton's shoulders and held on to him as waves of pleasure ran through my body.

"Easton," I whispered his name as his hand cupped my breast over my bra.

"I'm here, baby." His voice was soft, and his words were sweet, and for a second, I almost forgot what brought me to his room in the first place.

He unsnapped my bra, the lace falling to the floor, before his mouth left mine and traveled down my body. I audibly inhaled as he sucked my nipple into his mouth and Jemma sucked my earlobe in hers.

Easton continued down my body until he was on his knees in front of me, and I couldn't take my eyes off him as he lowered my panties to the ground helping me step out of them with my heels still on while Jemma continued to work her fingers against my clit.

I was so turned on, so fucking wet, and I needed him to do something, anything, before I fell apart right before his eyes.

His hands skimmed up my thighs, making them tremble under his touch, and I almost died when he looked up at me. His dark hair was disheveled, his eyes burned with need, and he kept them on me as he leaned down and buried his tongue in my pussy.

"Oh God." I gripped his head in my hands as his tongue moved over Jemma's fingers, and she turned my face toward hers and caught my lips in another kiss.

I cried into her mouth as her fingers gently spread me apart and Easton sucked my clit into his mouth. It was too much. I didn't want to come like this. I wanted Easton inside me. I didn't know if this would be the last time I was with him like this, and I knew that I couldn't walk out of this room until I felt him inside me at least one more time.

I pulled my mouth away from Jemma and looked down at Easton as he ate my pussy. "Please, Easton. I need you inside me."

His teeth nipped against my flesh, and I began to feel unsteady as my knees began to shake. Easton stood, wiping his mouth with the back of his hand, before wrapping that same hand around the back of my neck and kissing me like he was desperate.

I could taste myself on his lips, and I wondered if that was what Jemma would taste like. If she would be the same as me.

Easton helped me to the bed, my knees hitting the mattress right before the palms of my hands, and I heard the sound of his belt opening just as Jemma moved in front of me.

She kissed me again just as I felt Easton run his cock through my wet pussy, teasing my clit, and I moaned against her when he finally pushed inside.

Jemma moved her body in front of mine, her pussy on full

display in front of me, and I didn't have a fucking clue what to do. I had never been with a girl, never even kissed one before tonight, but Easton sensed my hesitation and leaned his chest against my back so he could whisper in my ear.

"Just think about what I do to you." He thrust inside me and my body moved forward an inch closer to hers. "Think about how I suck your clit into my mouth and how I fuck you with my fingers. You don't have to do anything you don't want to." I looked over my shoulder at him, and his lips moved against mine as he spoke. "I can tell her to leave. This can just be me and you."

I shook my head because I wasn't ready for her to leave. Not only because I was curious what this would be like, but also because I wasn't ready to be in this room alone with him. I wouldn't be able to handle him alone. I wouldn't survive him.

"Then just taste her," he whispered.

I moved between her legs, and she watched as I ran my tongue against her soft lips before dipping inside to find her clit. Easton was thrusting behind me, driving me forward onto her as I tasted her, driving me insane with lust.

I flicked my tongue over her clit, eliciting a deep moan from her just before I sucked her clit into my mouth like Easton had done so many times to me.

Jemma cupped her breasts, rolling her nipples, and I felt her whole body tensing. I dropped to my elbow as I arched my back, opening myself up more to Easton while using my free hand to touch her.

My pussy clenched around him as I spread her open with my fingers, and Jemma pushed her legs apart as she stared at me with her lip between her teeth. I ran my tongue over her, before pushing a finger inside her, and Easton groaned long and loud behind me.

I stared up at Jemma as I ate her, and I could feel her

orgasm climbing to the surface along with mine. Easton's hand found my clit as he began to thrust harder, and I shuddered against Jemma's pussy causing her to throw her head back with a moan.

It didn't take much longer before I was falling over the edge. I felt urgent and a little wild as I sucked on Jemma's flesh. Easton squeezed my clit between his fingers, and I fell hard. I screamed against Jemma and chased the high of my orgasm against her as I felt Easton come inside me.

She didn't last long after that. Her fingers dug into my hair, forcing me harder against her pussy, and I didn't let up until her thighs tightened around my head and she screamed out my name for anyone nearby to hear.

I laid my face against her thigh as I tried to come down from my orgasm, and Easton pressed a kiss to my back before he pulled out of me. I let my knees fall then, my stomach hitting the mattress, and as I heard him moving around his room cleaning up, my stomach tightened in nausea at what I had just done.

I pushed myself up and away from Jemma, but it had nothing to do with her and everything to do with him.

I would be lying if I said I didn't enjoy what just happened. I more than enjoyed it. But I hated that I would have never been confident enough to do something like this without him—without his encouragement, without that feeling that he wouldn't let me fall, but I was falling, and he was letting me.

And I was stupid enough to forget it for even a second.

I grabbed my panties from the floor and pulled them up my legs. I searched the floor for my bra, finally finding it under hers, and I snapped it in to place quickly.

"Maddison," Easton said my name as he moved toward me, but I was already scooping my dress off of the floor.

"Don't." I took a step back before pulling the dress over my head. I pressed my hand against my chest to hold the dress in place since I couldn't zip it myself, and I took another quick step toward the door.

"Maddison, please talk to me." His eyes searched my face, and I could tell he was panicking. He was losing me, and he knew it. Maybe he wasn't used to losing girls like this. I guess he was always the one to walk away.

"There's nothing to say, Easton." I could feel every ounce of tension from today building in my throat. "I got played." I shrugged my shoulders and turned for the door.

I had just turned the handle when he spoke again. "That guy you're running back to, the one who told you everything you need to know about me? He's the one who's playing you. He's the one that will break your heart. Not me."

Jemma was scurrying around the room, gathering her things when I looked back at Easton, but he wasn't paying her one bit of attention. He was only staring at me.

He had only touched me.

I would be lying if I said that there wasn't some part of me that doubted what Theo had said. But I had never not trusted my best friend, and I wasn't starting today.

"You already have."

His lips opened as he sucked in a breath, but I didn't stick around to hear what else he had to say. I pulled the door open and I hurried down the hall with my dress open behind me. I didn't stop moving until I got out of the house. I didn't care who saw me. I didn't care what they thought of me. All that mattered was getting out of this house that seemed to be smothering me.

I called Dillon as I hit the driveway, and she answered on the second ring.

"Where are you? We just got to the party." I could hear the

noise of the music and the dozens of people through the phone as I stared at the house.

"I need you." My voice cracked as I pressed the phone to my ear. "I'm outside."

"On my way." She breathed into the phone before hanging up, and when she appeared at the door a moment later, I finally let the first tear fall down my cheek.

CHAPTER 18

I HAD the biggest hangover of my life.

I wasn't sure if it was the alcohol or the way my chest felt like it was caving in on itself, but either way, I knew that surviving today would take everything inside me.

My eyes were puffy from crying most of the night, and I hated that there was some sort of physical evidence of my heartbreak. I was usually much better at hiding it.

I didn't have the energy or patience for my parents today, but I couldn't blow them off. I would never hear the end of it, and honestly, it wasn't worth it.

My phone dinged with a text message as I was getting ready for the game.

Easton: Please talk to me.

I read his words over and over, but I wasn't ready to face him again. I wasn't sure if I would ever be able to. So, I read the message repeatedly without sending a reply, but I pathetically hoped he'd send another.

I tugged a brush through my hair as I stared at my reflection in the mirror. I felt so different from the girl who walked into this dorm only a couple months ago, and it was hard to remember who I was then.

But she was still engraved in me. Deep down.

I was still the same girl that would never do anything to disappoint my parents or Theo for that matter, and I couldn't meet my own stare as I realized that.

I was pathetic, and I had let Easton convince me that I could be something different.

But I had been a fool.

I was nothing more than what I had always been.

My phone dinged again, and I scrambled to grab it off the dresser. I didn't know why I was disappointed when I saw a message from my mom letting me know they were here. Easton wasn't going to chase me. He wasn't going to be the guy who begged me to forgive him.

Because no matter how badly I wanted to believe it, he wasn't the guy I thought he was.

I straightened out the red dress my mother had bought me and looked at myself in the mirror one last time. I looked exactly like my mother would expect me to—exactly like she had trained me to look for most of my life.

And I fucking hated it.

I hated the way the fabric felt against my skin, I hated the way my normally wavy hair was perfectly straight, and I hated that I didn't feel an ounce of myself when I looked at me.

My parents were waiting in their car when I made my way outside, and I didn't miss the way my mother looked so similar to me as she waved through the windshield. I climbed into the backseat and smiled at Theo's dad who sat in the seat across from me.

"Hi, Mr. Hunt." I was happy he was here. I knew that Theo wanted to impress him more than anything, but it was hard to forget how badly I hated the man. He was cruel to Theo for most of his life, and regardless of how easily Theo swept all of that under the rug, I would not.

"Maddison, how are you?" He at least sounded sober, his words not slurring in the least, but I knew that wouldn't last very long. It never did.

"I'm great." I planted the fakest smile on my face, a smile I had mastered years ago, and met my mother's gaze in the rearview mirror.

My dad was typing away on his phone, and I had to stop myself from rolling my eyes. I hadn't seen him in weeks, and he still couldn't take the time to look up from that damn phone long enough to see me.

I felt like he never really saw me.

"Everyone ready?" My mom turned back toward me and my dad finally set his phone down on the console.

"All set."

My dad drove us through campus to the football stadium, and the traffic was absolutely insane. People were walking from the dorm fully decked out in red and black, and I wished I was with them instead of in that silent car with my parents and Theo's dad. My dad had a parking pass that got us right next to the stadium, and I suddenly felt like I hated everything.

Their car. Their parking space. Their season tickets that probably cost more than my tuition.

We climbed out of the car, and you could already hear the roar from the stadium as students and football fans started filling their seats. My head was pounding, and I could think of a million other places I'd rather be, most specifically my bed, but I would never do that to Theo.

I followed our parents into the stadium and through the crowds as we made our way to our seats. The student section was already packed, and I wished I was over there. I wished that I could go back just one day and that last night didn't happen. I could have come here with Easton. I wouldn't be sitting here wondering if he was here with someone else, I wouldn't be hating him as the thought crossed my mind.

"How are classes, Maddy?" My father leaned forward and spoke to me around my mother.

"They're fine." I wasn't lying. My classes were fine, but it wasn't really what he was asking. He wanted to know that I still had everything in perfect order, that I was still on his perfect plan.

"Good." He nodded just as Theo's dad took his seat next to him and handed him a beer. "Everyone around the office is missing you."

No one at that office missed me. They didn't care one thing

about me other than I was the boss' daughter, but I still smiled and nodded. "I miss them too."

He turned his attention to Mr. Hunt then and I huffed out a breath as I stared down at my phone. I considered texting Easton back. Telling him to stop texting me or to go to hell, but what I really wanted was for him to text me again.

I wanted to know what the hell he was thinking. I wanted to yell at him for making me fall for him and fucking up my head.

I just wanted... I didn't know what I wanted.

But I knew that every scenario I could think of included him.

"Here they come." My mother patted my leg, and I looked up just in time to watch the team run onto the field. I searched for Theo's number seven, but everything seemed like a blur of red and black from where I now stood with my parents. They were cheering, beyond excited to watch Theo finally start, and I tried to let some of their excitement rub off on me.

Theo had wanted this moment for forever, but all I could think about was Easton.

He had been all I had been able to think about since I met him.

My mom pointed to Theo, and I finally found him as they lined up on the field. The crowd went crazy with every play, but I could barely pay attention. Our parents kept talking about how well Theo was playing, and I watched as he scored the first touchdown of the game and the first of his college career. The stadium went wild with excitement just as the band started playing, and even though I was excited for Theo, I wanted to drown everything out. The noise, the chaos.

I pulled out my cellphone and searched for Easton's name on Instagram. There was picture after picture of him, and I tortured myself as I scrolled through them and tried to decipher which of the smiles he gave me seemed as real as the ones in the photos and which ones were nothing more than a ruse.

I clicked on his tagged photos, and I sat up straighter in my seat when I saw a picture of him that was posted by Oliver. They were at the game, this game, and even though I had no possible clue where he was, the fact that I knew he was here made my skin buzz.

I tucked my phone against my lap and tried to discretely search the student section for him, but it was no use. There were too many people. It was all a sea of red and black, and it was hard to decipher one face from the next.

"Do you want to run to the bathroom with me?" I looked up at my mom and realized it was already halftime. I had spent so much time worrying about Easton that I had missed almost half the game.

"Um, yeah." I stood from my seat and tugged on the end of my dress.

My mother and I followed the crowds of people who had a similar idea, and I searched every one of their faces looking for him.

"Theo is playing amazing." My mom turned to me when we got to the end of the bathroom line.

"He is," I answered her without barely paying her any attention.

"You seem distracted."

I finally looked up at her. "I've just been really busy with school."

"How was the formal last night?"

We both took a step forward as the line moved.

"It was fun," I lied. "Theo and I had a great time."

"Theo sent us a picture." She picked at a piece of lint of my dress as she spoke. "That's not the dress I would have picked for you, but you did look lovely."

I had to grind my teeth at her backhanded compliment. They were the only kind I typically got from her.

"Maddison." I heard Easton's voice, but I didn't turn toward him immediately. I didn't want to see him like this—not with her.

"Maddison," my mom said my name under her breath before gripping my arm and turning me in the direction of Easton.

"Oh. Hi, Easton." I attempted to force a smile on my face. "This is my mom. Mom, this is Easton. He's the TA for my English class."

His eyes narrowed slightly at my introduction, but I didn't care. I could feel my heart hammering against my chest, and I was worried that everyone around us could too.

Because he didn't look nearly as affected from last night as I was, but I'd be an idiot not to notice the way his blue eyes seemed more tired than usual. Actually, they looked exhausted.

"It's nice to meet you, Easton. I hope my Maddison has been a good student." She reached up and straightened the ends of my hair with her fingers.

"She's a great student." He didn't take his eyes off me. "We've been really impressed with her photojournalism skills as well. She has a real talent."

I could feel my mother straighten beside me and the urge to punch Easton right in front of her was overwhelming.

"She's a very talented girl." Her voice was much tighter than before, and I could hear the irritation in her voice.

"Maddison, do you think we can talk for a second?" Easton nodded his head to the side. "I have a few questions about our group project."

He was out of his mind if he thought that we were going to do this here.

"We can talk Monday." I stared at him and begged him

with my eyes not to do this. He had hurt me enough already. The least he could do was give me the decency to not hash it out in front of my mother.

He was watching me in a way that made me uneasy. I knew he didn't want to walk away from me, I could read it all over his face, but deep down there had to be some part of him that still cared enough about me that he didn't push it.

"Alright." He nodded his head, and I took a large thankful breath. "I'll text you." He looked down at the phone in my hand, making it clear that he knew I was ignoring his texts. "It was very nice to meet you, Mrs. Duncan. I hope you know how special your girl is."

He didn't give my mother time to respond as he turned and walked away from us. I watched his back as he ran his hands through his hair in frustration, and I wanted to go to him.

Even after everything, I wanted to make sure he was okay.

"He's handsome."

I looked up at my mom as we took another step toward the bathroom. "He is."

"What was he talking about with the photography?" She was digging through her purse as she asked the question, but I knew she was dying for the answer. My parents made it perfectly clear what they thought about my dream of photojournalism.

"It was just for a project. No big deal," I lied through my teeth. It was a huge deal that Easton had bought me my first camera. At the time, I thought it meant more than it did. I thought I meant more than I did.

"Okay. Oh, the bathroom's finally open."

I locked myself inside a stall as soon as we walked in and tried to breathe through the panic I could feel rising. Easton had made me believe that I could have things that I never thought was possible before. He had fooled me in so many ways.

Breaking my heart apparently wasn't good enough for him.

He knew what my parents thought about Columbia, what they thought about photojournalism. He was the only one I had ever told, and I didn't need him throwing it back in my face now that he no longer cared.

My parents would stop supporting me.

And just the thought scared the crap out of me. I knew that made me a coward. Easton supported himself and worked his ass off to be where he was, but I wasn't like Easton. I didn't know if I could feed myself without my parents' help let alone do everything on my own.

I was scared I couldn't do it without them. Without Theo.

And now without him.

...

"Theo, that was a great game." My father clapped Theo on the back as we sat down for dinner, and I had to fight back the urge to roll my eyes. My father had already talked to Theo more in the last five minutes since he arrived than he did to me the entire game.

"Thank you, Mr. Duncan. It felt good."

Theo had two touchdowns, a hundred rushing yards, and some other statistic that our parents couldn't stop talking about.

"I bet you get drafted during your junior year," my mother bragged, but Theo's dad scoffed around the glass of whiskey that was currently pressed to his lips.

My mother straightened but didn't say another word. She was really good at that.

So was my father.

I used to be, but something had changed. Normally, I

would look across the table at Theo and give him a sympathetic look and we'd talk about it later. But I was so over that.

"You don't think Theo is going to be drafted?" I looked right at his father as I said the words, and I didn't look away as his gaze burned into mine.

"I didn't say that. I just think he has a lot of work to put in." He took another long sip of his drink, and I knew from his glassy-eyed expression that he was well on his way to drunk.

"Your son's incredible."

Theo was stock still across from me, but for the first time in my whole life, I didn't care if he was uncomfortable. I couldn't sit by and watch his father do this. Not anymore.

"I never said that he wasn't." Mr. Hunt tried to dismiss me as he smiled over at my father.

"But you never said he was either."

"Maddison." My father's stern voice tugged at me to be quiet, to stop what I was doing, but I didn't.

"Dad." I met his stare head-on, something I never did, and I could feel my hands shaking under the table.

"Maddy, let's go get some air." I finally looked away from my father to see Theo standing beside me with his hand reached out to me. I didn't want to take his hand and walk outside like I wasn't upset. I didn't want to do things exactly like we had always done, but I was still raw from last night and I knew that I was willing to let myself take things too far.

I placed my hand in his and his fingers tightened around mine as he helped me from my chair. Our parents didn't utter a word, and I could just imagine the way my mother would apologize for my behavior once we were outside.

But I didn't need anyone apologizing for me.

We walked outside, and I took a deep breath once we left the stifling air of the restaurant.

"Maddy." Theo said my name like he was trying to figure out what to say to me.

"I'm sorry." I gripped the balcony rail in my hands and turned toward him. "I know you don't need me defending you."

He looked up at me then, his face suddenly serious. "I'll always need you."

"That's not what I meant." I rolled my eyes. "I mean when it comes to—"

I didn't get to finish my sentence because Theo stopped it with his lips. I took a deep shuddering breath as his lips pressed against mine, and Theo shifted to get even closer to me. His body pressed against mine, his hand tangled in my hair.

He didn't care that we were on the balcony of some restaurant. He dove into me as if it were only me and him, and it felt like it always had been.

I had dreamed of this moment for so long that I didn't know what to do. I was stiff in his arms—hesitant and scared. Theo traced his tongue along the seam of my lips, and I opened them on a shocked breath just before he slipped inside.

His tongue touched mine, and I finally kissed him back. I rolled my tongue against his, I gripped his arms in my fingers, and I searched for what I needed in everything that he was.

I pulled him tighter against me, and he groaned as our hips met through our clothes. One of his hands clung to my hip while the other remained tangled in my hair, and I pressed myself closer against him to try to chase the feeling I needed. I needed more and not because I was desperate for it, but because I was desperate for this to feel like more than it did with Easton.

Theo's hand helped guide me as his thigh slipped between my legs and I chased the feeling I so helplessly wanted through our clothes. The feeling that Easton brought out in me with a single touch.

"Fuck, Maddy," Theo whispered the words against my lips, and I bit his bottom lip and forced his mouth back against mine.

If I was with Easton, he would have already taken control and had my stomach in knots by the feelings he would have created in me. He would be gripping my hips, his hand would be roaming my body, his mouth exploring my neck. But Theo wasn't doing any of that.

I pulled his hand from my hair and brought it to my breast. He cupped the weight in his hand, his hand hidden between us as his thumb brushed over my nipple through my bra, but I wanted him to do something more. I wanted him to grip me through the fabric in a way that made me feel like there was nothing between us. I wanted him to do something. To make me feel something more.

"We should get back inside," he murmured against my mouth, but I didn't care about getting back to our parents.

I had waited what felt like half my life for this kiss.

I brought my mouth back to his and kissed him. It was just as passionate as before, just as desperate for him to give me more. I rolled my hips against his, and I could feel how hard he was against my leg. I knew he wanted me, and even if I felt nothing like I did when I was with Easton, I still wanted Theo. I wanted him to show me what we could be. What we had been missing for so long.

He groaned against my mouth and shifted his hips against me.

"Your parents." Theo groaned, and I finally let my mouth fall from his and I dropped my forehead to his chest.

I had an overwhelming urge to cry or scream or possibly punch something, and I hated how out of control I felt. This moment with Theo was supposed to be perfect.

It would have been perfect before Easton, before everything that happened, but now everything was completely fucked up.

"You're right." I nodded my head against his chest. "We should go back inside."

He ran his fingers through my hair and lifted my face until I couldn't see anything but him.

"Are you okay?"

I hated myself for thinking about Easton in that moment.

Theo Hunt was the guy of my dreams, and now that those dreams were finally coming true, I was wishing he was someone else.

"I'm okay," I lied, but Theo smiled at me like he believed it.

And I hated myself for that even more.

CHAPTER 19

I HAD no idea what I was doing.

I didn't answer Theo when he called last night after our parents dropped me off at my dorm. I didn't know what to say to him, how to go back to what we were before.

I didn't answer Easton either.

There was another text message this morning. Another **Please talk to me**. But I was so fucking confused that I didn't know what to say to either of them.

I had wanted Theo for so long that I had barely thought about anything else, but Easton changed everything. Everything before Easton made sense.

But he had me questioning everything.

Every decision I made before Easton was affected by someone else. Whether it was my parents or Theo or the thought of what others would think of me, I never made a decision simply for myself. And it never seemed to matter until him.

But now? Now my skin was itching with the urge to run. To get away from this school. From everyone.

But I knew I couldn't.

My stomach was in knots as I walked into my English class on Monday. I spotted Easton in his spot behind Professor Bryant's desk before I even made it through the doorway, and I didn't know how I was going to make it through the entire class without falling apart.

I could feel him watching me as I took my seat, but I refused to look in his direction. I wouldn't be able to handle it.

Imani was already drawing in her seat next to me, and she looked up long enough to smile before she went back to her work. I pulled out my notebook, textbook, and pencil and laid them out on my desk. When Professor Bryant still hadn't entered the room, I took out my phone so I would have something to distract me.

There were two text messages on my phone as I lit it up. One of them just arrived a moment ago.

Theo: Want to hang out tonight?

Easton: You're fucking gorgeous.

I finally looked up at him then, and he was already staring at me. I didn't know what he wanted from me. What he wanted me to say. Did he expect a thank you?

Did he want me to come crawling back to him?

Whatever it was that he wanted, I wasn't able to give it to him.

I put my phone away without replying to either, and I stared at the whiteboard until Professor Bryant walked in with a stack of papers in his hands.

"Good morning," he said loudly, causing the chatter in the room to quiet. "I have your papers graded. Some of you did excellent. Some of you would have done better if you hadn't turned anything in."

The class laughed as the professor handed the papers to Easton, and he stood from his seat.

I tried not to watch him as he began passing out everyone's paper, but it was impossible. He was wearing a black t-shirt and a pair of deep grey shorts, and I hated the way all the girls ogled him as he walked by.

I wanted to yell at them and tell them that he was mine, but he wasn't.

Even if he was, he couldn't be.

I forced myself to face forward and watch Professor Bryant. He was still talking, but I wasn't hearing a thing he was saying. I was too focused on steadying my breath, on calculating how close Easton was to me.

"Your group projects are due this week." A round of groans rang out through the room. "Remember that it counts for fifteen percent of your grade, so starting to work on it today isn't going to be the best idea."

I felt Easton behind me, I could smell the hint of spice from his cologne, and I tensed as he set my paper down in front of me. His arm grazed mine. It would look innocent to anyone else, but I knew better.

Easton knew exactly what he was doing to me.

He always had.

I didn't know what I was expecting after everything that had happened, but I wanted to be able to forget Easton. I wanted to pretend that there was nothing between us but sexual tension and a track record of really good sex.

But I couldn't even manage to lie to myself, let alone anyone else.

"I'm going to give you today to meet with your partner and work on finalizing your project."

I finally looked up at the professor and heard the words he was saying.

"You can pair up in here. Some of you can go out into the hall. Wherever you can find some quiet space, but no one leaves until class is over." He pointed his finger at all of us. "You're welcome."

The class laughed and shifted in their seats as they moved to find their partner. I didn't move an inch. I stared ahead of me and tried not to panic.

I didn't want to talk to Easton. Not even about our stupid group project that I had already finished, but what was I going to say.

No thank you. I don't want to work with your TA because he broke my fucking heart.

Easton set the rest of the papers in his hand down on the desk before looking up at me. He started talking to the professor, but I could hear every word.

"I'm going to take the rest of these to your office. We'll work in there if that's cool with you."

Professor Bryant nodded. "It will definitely be quieter in there. There's a letter on my desk for you too."

"Thanks." Easton smiled at him before turning back to me.

"You ready?" He nodded toward the door.

I was so pissed at him. I didn't want to go to the professor's office with him. I didn't want to be within five feet of him, but he knew I wouldn't refuse him in front of the professor—in front of the entire class.

I gathered my things in my arms and stood before moving out the door with Easton trailing me. I had no idea where Professor Bryant's office was, but Easton started walking toward the right and I followed him.

He unlocked the professor's office and set the papers down on his desk as I made my way into the room. I didn't dare close the door behind me. I could hardly breathe as it was.

He turned toward me and leaned against the desk.

"We're finished with our project," I told him something that he already knew. "Is it necessary for me to stay for the entire class?"

"The professor said so." He shrugged his shoulders, and I could tell he was fighting a smirk.

"Well, the professor isn't the one who's been fucking me, so I'm asking you."

He pushed off the desk and quickly closed the door before someone overheard me, and it completely pissed me off.

I knew I had no business getting so worked up, the two of us barely even knew each other, but it was impossible to tell your heart not to care.

And Easton had made me care too much.

"I don't know what the fuck Theo told you, but I didn't do anything."

"Theo wouldn't lie to me." I shook my head.

"Wouldn't he?" He cocked his head to the side. "Theo only wants you to himself. He would do anything to get me away from you."

"I don't have time for this." I headed toward the door, but he pressed his back against mine and stopped me from turning the handle.

"Just give me a chance, Maddison. Don't I deserve a fucking chance?" His voice was rough and vulnerable and made me want to give in to everything he wanted. It made me want to give him everything that I was.

"For what?" I pressed my hand against the door to help steady myself. "We couldn't be together even if we wanted to. You're my fucking TA, Easton." I turned toward him and waved my hand around the professor's office. "Did you happen to forget that little detail? Just leave me alone. It's for the best."

"I can't." He sounded as broken as I felt, and I hated him for it.

My back slammed into the wall as his mouth crashed into mine.

I didn't have time to think about whether what we were doing was right or wrong. All I knew was that one single touch from him, and I was already feeling everything I had been chasing from Theo yesterday.

And the thought made me sick, but I couldn't stop.

He lifted me, my thighs wrapping around him instantly, and something crashed to the ground around us. Easton didn't seem to notice or care. He was too busy dragging his mouth down my neck with the press of his tongue and the nip of his teeth, and I couldn't catch my breath as he set me down on the desk.

I felt so engulfed by him. So completely lost in everything that he was that it didn't matter if he had been using me. It didn't matter that I was falling in love with him when he didn't feel the same.

His hand fumbled with the button of my jeans in his haste, and I helped him pull them down my legs before sitting against the desk once more. His jeans were undone just as quickly, and we didn't waste any time.

I was clawing at his skin trying to get closer to him as he pushed inside me. I fell back on my hands, trying to support myself against his thrusts, but it was useless. I dropped to my back, papers flying to the floor behind me, and I held onto the edge of the desk as he thrust into me over and over.

Every inch of my skin was dying for his touch, and Easton knew it. His hand thrust up my shirt and he rolled my nipple through my bra, and I was forced to put a hand over my mouth to keep from crying out.

I was so lost in him as he leaned forward and gripped my chin in his hand. I kissed him like he hadn't hurt me. Like everything about the two of us wasn't a bad idea. Not a trace of those rules or that hurt was between us now. It was only me and him, and I fell apart around him as his lips pressed against mine like he was desperately trying to hold on to this moment forever.

My orgasm raked through my body without warning or control. It was a wild shock of passion and need, and something inside me broke as it tore through every inch of me.

I could feel Easton's own orgasm spill from him inside of me, and I tried to breathe as a tear slid down my face. I didn't give him time to recover as I pushed his chest away from mine. I could feel my panic crawling up my skin, taking up every inch of where pleasure had just been, and I knew that I had made a mistake.

I climbed off his desk and jerked my jeans up my legs as he

looked at me with the same look of panic on his face. I grabbed my things from the floor and jerked the door open in haste.

Because I was never going to recover from Easton Cole.

He was destroying every piece of me, and I was letting him.

CHAPTER 20

GOING to Theo's house was probably the worst idea I had ever had, but I needed my friend. I needed the person he was to me before everything that happened yesterday. He had been my everything for so long that I didn't know how to break the habit.

I didn't know how to stop him.

He was sitting at his desk when I walked in, but he smiled as soon as he saw me.

"Hi." He turned in his chair to face me, and I walked toward him with my heart beating wildly in my chest.

I wished I could stop it, that feeling, but there was something about Theo that had always made me feel like I was constantly falling.

But that beat that used to feel like thunder somehow slowed to a rainstorm, and no matter how hard I tried, everything with Theo felt like a tremble compared to the earth-shattering effect of Easton.

"Hi." I stopped a good foot away from him, but he reached out and pulled me closer to him without hesitation.

My thighs were between his, and he was smiling at me like I was the best thing he had seen all day. I felt like the worst kind of person. Worse than Easton. Worse than anything Theo could ever do to me.

He tried to pull me down toward him. I could see him watching my lips, but I couldn't kiss him after kissing Easton.

After I had just fucked Easton not even an hour before.

"Wait." I pulled away from him. I pulled away from the thing I had wanted for most of my life and looked up at my best friend. "I need to tell you something."

"Okay." He chuckled and ran his thumb over my bent knee.

"I applied to Columbia before here." I pointed down as if I was actually talking about the room we were standing in.

"Okay..." He still had a small smile on his face, but his brow was bunched in confusion.

"I got accepted. To Columbia," I said it again to make sure he heard me. "I was offered a full scholarship for photo-journalism."

"I'm confused." He sat up straighter and looked at me. "Why are you telling me this? You've never been interested in photojournalism before. I thought you wanted to work for your dad."

"I don't." I shook my head and tried to figure out what I was trying to say. "My parents want me to work for my dad. My parents wanted me to go here. You wanted me to go here. I tried to tell you before, but you were so excited about us being here together, and I didn't know how to say it."

"So what?" He scooted away from me and I felt him pull away in more ways than one. "Now you want to be a photojournalist? Can you even do that?"

I jolted back as if he had slapped me. "Yes, Theo. I can. If we talked about me instead of football for more than five seconds, maybe you would already know that."

I could see him grind his jaw, but he didn't respond to my dig.

"So study photojournalism here." He held his arms out around him. "I don't understand what the big deal is."

"I just wanted to tell you." I stepped another step away from him and ran my finger over his desk. "I wanted to know what you'd say. What you'd think."

"I think your dad's going to be pissed. Why wouldn't you stick to the plan that's perfectly laid out in front of you instead of wasting these years, all this education, on something that you could fail at? Did Easton talk you into this?"

I pulled the sleeves of my shirt around the palms of my hands. "No. Easton has nothing to do with this."

"Of course he does." He stood and started pacing the room. "All he ever talks about is getting into grad school, and I know that he has a meeting scheduled with one of the professors at Columbia. I overheard him talking about it."

This was news to me. "I didn't know that."

"Don't try to fuck with me, Maddison." He ran his fingers through his hair. "I don't know what you want. I thought this was what you wanted." He pointed between me and him.

"I thought it was too." I nodded, and I could feel my throat closing around the words.

"So what now?" He was so angry. I had never seen him this upset. "Now you want to run away to Columbia with Easton and forget everything that we've had together."

"Of course not. Easton has nothing to do with Columbia," I said, getting frustrated with the conversation.

"You fucked him. Didn't you?" He was staring at me like he didn't know who I was.

"What?" My heart was racing, and I just wanted this to stop. "That's none of your business, Theo. Just like that girl at the formal was none of mine."

"This is my business." He took a step toward me, and I held my breath. "Easton is my frat brother and your fucking TA, Maddy. He should have never got involved with you."

"Give me a break, Theo. He's not my professor. He's a student." I was tired of hearing about Easton being my TA as if it made him some untouchable god. I knew there were rules, but I didn't care. We hadn't done anything wrong. At least, I hadn't.

"And he chose to fuck the wrong one."

I was shocked by the venom in his voice.

"Are you kidding me, Theo? What are you going to do, fight him?" I rolled my eyes. "I called him out on playing me. I'm not going to be seeing him again."

"I don't care about that." He practically growled.

"You don't care?" My brow scrunched in confusion and I could feel heat crawling up my chest in frustration. "You're the one who told me. You're the one who made me push him away."

"He never deserved you, Maddison. You are mine. You were mine way before he met you."

I turned on him then, my heart racing in anger. I had wanted to be Theo's for so damn long, and now, here he was laying some sort of claim on me like this.

"I'm confused." I crossed my arms. "Am I not supposed to be with Easton because he was playing me or because he's my TA or because you just don't want me to?"

Theo looked at me then, really looked at me, and I could see it all in his eyes. The only one playing me had been him, and I had ruined everything on the word of my best friend. I had ruined everything because he wanted me for himself when he had never really wanted me at all.

"Maddy." He reached out and touched my arm, but I jerked out of his touch.

"Answer me, Theo."

"Your parents will never let you go to Columbia." He shook his head. "Your dad will never allow it."

"I don't give two fucks what my dad will allow. We're not talking about my dad, Theo. We're talking about us."

"What do you want, Maddison? You were dry humping me like whatever Easton had been doing to you hadn't ever hit the spot two days ago and today you're telling me that you have some wild hair to take pictures. You're going to ruin everything. You and I are end game, Maddy. I've known it for forever and so have you."

I could barely breathe as he spoke. "So what? You get to

run around with any girl you want, fucking anyone you want, until you decided to let me in on this little secret of yours?"

"It's not a secret. It's a plan." He ran his fingers through his hair in frustration, and I realized that he was being serious. "These other girls don't matter. You matter. I thought I wanted to wait until at least my senior year before we settled down together, but I was wrong. I don't want to wait."

"You have a plan." I said the words out loud, but I was trying to get them through my own head. I was trying to understand how my best friend thought I was some variable of his perfect life plan.

"Yes." He reached out for me but dropped his hand when he saw my face. "After we graduate and move back home, we'd get married. Your dad's told me a hundred times that he'd love to have me as a son-in-law."

I didn't even realize I was doing it until my hand connected with his face. He looked as shocked as I felt, and I didn't even know what to say. The words *I'm sorry* had no risk of passing my lips because I wasn't.

"Fuck you and your plan." I moved toward the door, and I hated the sinking feeling that seemed to overtake me. "You're an asshole, Theo."

For the first time since I had known him, Theo was no longer the one who could protect me when my life started falling apart around me.

And I felt another piece of my heart break as I left his room and didn't look back.

CHAPTER 21

I HADN'T TALKED to Easton or Theo in over three days.

Although I knew it was best to give me time away from both of them, there was an ache deep in my chest that made me miss them both.

I missed them differently, but I missed them both, all the same.

I didn't even know what I would say to Easton. How I would make things right.

Dillon knew everything. Everything that had happened between Easton and me, everything with Theo, and she had to talk me off the ledge a couple times.

But she sat beside me on my bed as my phone rang six times before I finally reached the secretary of the admissions department at Columbia University. She didn't move an inch as I spoke with one of the admissions counselors about my scholarship and the slim chance I may have had of transferring to Columbia for the next semester.

My heart was racing as the admissions counselor talked about their policies and how she would have to speak with someone within the journalism department before a decision could be made, but all I could think about was Easton.

Without him, I would have never called.

Without him, I would have never been brave enough to even think I could do this.

Even though everything with us seemed impossibly fucked up, he taught me that trying to be what other people thought I should be was a waste. I only had one life, and so far, I had been living it for everyone except me.

I hung up the phone and looked at Dillon. "They're going to call me back."

"That's good, right? They didn't say no."

"Right." I nodded even though I didn't feel as confident as she did.

There was a loud knock on our door, an insistent pounding, and Dillon and I looked at each other before she stood and opened the door to our small dorm room.

"Where is Maddison?" I heard Easton's voice, a voice filled with anger, and I leaned forward on my bed to see him filling the doorway with Dillon blocking his path. "Where is she?" he asked again before giving Dillon a chance to respond.

"Easton." I stood from the bed where he could see me, and his eyes burned with anger when he did.

He pushed past Dillon, not caring one bit, and he was so close to me as the next words left his mouth. "I can't believe you." He cleared his throat as if he was trying to rein himself in. "I can't believe that I let you in, that I let myself fall in love with you."

I inhaled, an audibly shocked breath, at his words, and my heart felt like it was about to beat out of my chest.

"How could you?"

He had every right to be mad at me. I was mad at myself, but I was still surprised by his anger. It had been days since I had ruined everything. It had been days since I chose Theo over him.

"I'm sorry." I shook my head as my voice began to shake. "I should have talked to you. What Theo told me—"

"I don't give a fuck about Theo." His voice boomed through the room, and I took a step back. "I trusted you. I told you things I had never told anyone."

"We can figure this out." I stepped toward him, but he escaped my touch as if I'd burn him as he laughed.

"So, what? You thought you'd cause me to lose my TA position then we'd run off into the sunset?"

His words hit me like a ton of bricks. "What are you talking about?"

"Don't act stupid, Maddison. You're too damn smart for that."

Dillon had left the room, and I didn't blame her. His anger was stifling.

"I don't know what you're talking about, Easton. What happened?" I wasn't lying. I had no idea what he was talking about, but he was looking at me like I was the biggest liar he had ever met.

And maybe I was.

"I fucked with the wrong girl apparently." He threw his arms out to his sides, and Theo's words rang through my head.

And he chose to fuck the wrong one.

I pressed my hand against my chest and tried to catch my breath. "Easton, I didn't." I shook my head. "I would never."

"I don't care anymore, Maddison." He shook his head and stepped back from me. "I thought you were different. I thought you were special. Turns out, you were the one taking advantage of me."

Hatred filled his expression, and even though I regretted the fact that I was the one who put it there, I couldn't look away.

I didn't look away when the door to my dorm room opened and Dillon said my name with worry.

And I didn't look away when I heard her curse under her breath when Theo pushed past her.

"Maddy," Theo said my name with desperation on his lips, and it was clear he knew that I was aware of what he'd done.

That I knew he'd betrayed me.

"Are you fucking kidding me?" Easton turned in Theo's direction, but I reached my hand out against his arm to stop him. His gaze jerked to where my skin touched his before he finally looked back up at me. "Are you two finally at thing?" He pointed his hand between me and Theo. "After all the shit he's put you through?"

"Fuck you, dude." Theo took a step toward Easton, but there was no way in hell I was letting the two of them fight. Not over me.

I stepped in front of Easton, and Theo's hostile stare dropped to me.

"You need to leave." I could barely believe the words coming out of my mouth. "I'll call you later."

He jolted back as if I had slapped him and pointed to his chest. "Me. You want me to leave?"

"What did you do, Theo?" I just needed some honesty from him. One moment of honesty in what felt like a sea of tiptoeing around the truth.

"You're not supposed to be with him, Maddy."

I felt Easton's already tense body go stock still behind me.

"I wasn't going to sit by and watch him take advantage of you."

Easton started to say something, but I didn't let him. "Get out."

Theo looked as shocked as I felt. "You're choosing him over me?" He narrowed his eyes, and I despised everything about this Theo. This guy in front of me wasn't the same guy who had been my best friend for the past six years. He wasn't the guy I had fallen in love with.

"No." I shook my head, and even though I knew Easton probably felt the same about me as I did about Theo in that moment, I used the strength of him behind me to say my next words. "I'm choosing me."

Theo stared at me, and I counted to ten in my head before he finally looked behind me to Easton. Easton didn't say a word. He didn't move an inch. He just stood behind me and let Theo take his fill.

Theo turned to leave as his eyes met mine again, and I saw it then, the urge to say he was sorry, the urge to make things right. But I knew he wouldn't do it here.

Not in front of Easton.

Not when I was asking him to leave and for Easton to stay.

He jerked the door open, and when it closed behind him, I felt his absence instantly.

Regardless of who I chose, I knew my heart was going to break either way.

I was in love with two different men.

And I could only have one.

But the one I wanted was still looking at me like I was a mistake, and even though he had said he was falling for me, I feared that the two of us didn't fall the same.

Falling for Easton felt like I was falling again and again. There was no end in sight. No life raft to help bring me back to the surface for a quick pull of air.

But he looked like he was breathing fine.

"I should go." He didn't move even after he said the words. He was staring down at me, and I knew that he wanted to say more. I begged him to say more.

"Please don't." I reached out for his hand, but his fingers slipped through mine before I could ever grip them. "I'll fix this."

"It's too late." He held his arms out to his sides, and that small moment where his anger had slipped away was gone. "I'm not like you and Theo. My position, my scholarship, that was all that I had. I wasn't born with a silver spoon in my mouth."

His words stung, but they were true, and I deserved them.

I was fucking up everything for him. I had fucked up everything.

"I'm sorry." My voice cracked as I said the only thing I knew to say.

Easton shook his head, and I knew that it was the last thing he wanted to hear from me. He moved toward the door, the same door Theo had just left through, but he hesitated.

"I'm sorry too. You know?" He didn't wait for my reply. Before I could even muster up the courage to ask him to stay, he was gone.

CHAPTER 22

IT FELT odd coming to the frat house without Theo or Easton at my side. But I hadn't spoken to either of them. Not a single call. Not a measly text. Nothing.

I didn't knock on the door before entering. There were a couple guys sitting in the living room when I walked by, but I didn't pay them any attention. I wasn't here for them.

I climbed up the stairs and knocked on the third door to the left. At first, I didn't think he was there, but I knew that his car was in the driveway and practice ended hours ago. After a couple minutes, his door finally opened, and my best friend stood on the other side.

I adjusted the strap of my bag on my shoulder and looked up at him for the first time in days. "I talked to Professor Bryant."

"You did?" His hand was still on the door, and I wasn't sure if he wanted me to come in or not, but I didn't care.

I pushed past him and set my bag down on his desk as he closed the door behind him.

"He told me that you came and talked to him."

He ran his hand over the back of his head, and I hated how uneasy he looked. We were never like this with each other. "I don't know if it helped. I just... I just regretted what I did. I shouldn't... I'm sorry."

It had helped. When I barged into Professor Bryant's office, the same office I had been in with Easton just a few days before, he told me that Easton was fired from his position. I begged him to change his decision. I lied. I told him that Easton and I were nothing more than friends, a position he had forced us into when he paired us up as group project partners.

He didn't let me get much further than that. He held his hand up to cut me off. He told me that Theo had retracted what he said about Easton, that he said he had made a mistake, but it was too late.

Easton lost his TA position, but the professor assured me that it wouldn't affect his scholarships.

And even though I knew that didn't change everything, I still breathed easier than I had moments before I walked in.

"You've been a shitty friend, Theo."

"I know." The words rushed out of him.

"But so have I."

His eyes searched mine.

"I shouldn't have lied to you about Easton. I should have been honest with you from the beginning. About everything. Easton, school, Columbia."

He nodded, but he still looked like someone kicked his puppy. "Can we make up? I've felt like shit the last couple days not talking to you."

I smiled because I knew the feeling. Theo had been an integral part of my life for so long, and no other guy would be able to change that. No other guy would be able to replace him.

"We can, but I need to tell you something first."

"You and Easton?" He cocked his head to the side, but he didn't seem nearly as upset as I would have expected.

I shook my head at his assumption. "We haven't talked. I need to tell you about school. I'm transferring to Columbia at the end of this semester."

"What?"

"I heard back from them yesterday. They're going to honor the original scholarship they offered me."

He watched me for a second and I could see him trying to figure out what to say to me.

"You're sure about this?"

"I am." I felt more sure about this decision than I ever had before.

"And your parents?" He winced as he said it. Whether it

was because he knew I wouldn't want to talk about them or because he knew what their reaction would be, I didn't know.

"They're pissed." I shrugged my shoulders. "Dad said he won't support me, and I told him that I'd get a job."

Theo laughed, a loud boisterous sound, and I couldn't help but join in. "I bet that went over well."

"They were scrambling after that." I shrugged. "But they had nothing left to threaten me with."

"So, New York?" He finally moved closer to me and sat down on the bed in front of me.

"Yeah. I hear I still get good reception for Facetime there."

"Yeah?" He grinned and every ounce of anger I had toward him melted away.

"Yeah. My best friend is a bit needy."

"But he's still your best friend?" He looked up, and he looked so unsure of himself.

"Forever."

CHAPTER 23

MY PARENTS WERE FREAKING OUT.

Their perfect little daughter with her perfect hair and perfect clothes on the perfect life path was officially screwing everything up.

But I didn't care.

My dad was furious when I told him that I would figure everything out after he threatened to cut me off. It was the only leverage they had over me now, and neither of them thought I was strong enough to do it on my own.

But I would prove them wrong.

In the week since everything happened, I was already fully enrolled in Columbia University for the spring semester. My scholarship covered one hundred percent of my tuition, but nothing else. Student housing was more expensive there than it was at The University of Georgia, but Theo spent hours with me going over different student loan options and deciding which one was right for me.

I felt settled somehow.

Everything in my life felt like it was off track, every decision that had been made for me for so long had gone askew, but somehow I felt more secure than I had in a long time.

I still hadn't spoken to Easton.

I called him, twice, and send him a text, but he didn't respond to any of it.

I didn't know what to say to him. I didn't know if there was anything I could do that would change what had happened between us.

But I knew that I couldn't stay here for him. Not that he even wanted me to.

I slid my phone into my back pocket as I jogged down the stairs. There was a barbecue at the Kappa frat house tonight, and I figured I had been avoiding the place for long enough. I was bound to run into Easton one way or another, and I couldn't stop hanging out with my best friend for fear that I would.

It didn't matter anyway. As soon as I pushed open the door to our dorms, I spotted him in the parking lot leaning against the driver's side door of my car. He watched me as I walked toward him, but I couldn't take my eyes off his white t-shirt that read Columbia University across the chest in blue.

Shivers ran through me the closer I got to him. I knew seeing him would be hard, but this was different. My whole body felt like it was on fire as I walked toward him. I could feel the flames licking up my skin, but I was no longer afraid of being burned.

"What are you doing here?" I looked from one side to the next, anywhere but directly at him, and I wrapped my arms around myself.

"I heard a rumor about you, Ms. Duncan." He was still leaning back against my car. He looked so calm and confident, and for a moment, I wished that I could take away everything that had happened between us. I wished he were just a boy and I was just a girl and that the world was still at our fingertips.

"Which rumor would that be?" My eyes finally met his blue ones. "There seems to be a few going around."

He smirked then, that cocky self-assured smirk that I couldn't get enough of, and I knew that a week away from him had done nothing but made me weaker against him.

"I heard that you're leaving for New York." He cocked his head to the side, just slightly, and waited for my answer.

"I am." I nodded, and for some reason, I was more nervous to tell Easton about Columbia than anyone.

"This will definitely be a story for our children." He pushed off the car and took a step toward me. "Their mom planned to leave me without a single word, and she didn't even think that I would follow her."

I sucked in a broken breath, and he kept talking.

"She didn't think that after everything that I would still love her. That I would do whatever it took to figure everything out."

I shook my head because I couldn't even comprehend what he was saying. He wasn't supposed to forgive me. I had no right to his forgiveness. "Easton."

"But she was wrong." He stood directly in front of me now. The tip of his shoes touching mine. "I should have called you back, but I needed some time."

I stared at him as I nodded, but he didn't owe me any explanation. "I didn't expect you to call me back."

"I didn't expect you to go to Columbia." His voice was softer now.

I shrugged my shoulders like it was no big deal, but we both knew it was. "And what about you? What now since you lost your TA position?"

"Well." He reached his hand out and wrapped his fingers around my hip before pulling me a step closer to him. "It turns out the perks of the job weren't as good as I thought."

"No?" I was staring up at him, but he was staring at my lips.

"No. I mean the professor's letter of recommendation helped me get accepted to Columbia for grad school next fall, but I'm not sure how much that matters if I can't date the students."

I wanted to laugh, even with every inch of my body feeling like a live wire in his touch. "You have any specific students in mind?"

The grin that lit up his face was the grin of a heartbreaker, and I knew firsthand just how treacherous falling for him could be.

He didn't give me time to catch my breath or to calm down my heart. He reached forward, wrapping his other hand around my neck, and he kissed me like he had been missing me as badly as I had been missing him.

It wasn't gentle or teasing. It felt like a storm. The wild chaos of lightning and wind and rain pounding down against me, and just for a second there was a silence, just before the thunder hit, and I knew with absolute certainty that I would never love anyone like I loved Easton Cole.

He pulled away from me, and I was terrified.

Loving someone like that was scary, and I knew that he would demand all of me.

But I was tired of living with both feet planted firmly on the ground. I was ready to take the plunge and go all in. No excuses. No one to decide but me and him.

Easton pressed his lips back against mine, gently this time, and he whispered his words against my lips.

"Just one."

THE END

EPILOGUE

EASTON

Three Months Later

I NEVER REALLY THOUGHT THAT I would be visiting my girlfriend at the same school I had been working my ass off to get into for the last four years.

If you had told me I'd be here six months ago, I wouldn't have believed you. I wouldn't have believed any of it.

But here I was climbing up the steps of Maddison's new dorm room, and all I could think about was her. Hell, the only thing I had been able to think about since Maddison Duncan walked into my chest was her.

I never stood a chance.

Not when she arrived at The University of Georgia and not when she left.

It didn't matter where she was. I wanted her, and now that she was officially mine, I wouldn't let anything get between us again.

Not her parents who already didn't like me even though they didn't know shit about me.

Not some stupid rules school rules.

And definitely not Theo Hunt.

Maddison had forgiven him so easily—too easily if you asked me, but I was still working on it. I had a feeling I was going to be working on it for a while. But he was her best friend, and for her, I was willing to try anything.

I knocked on the old wooden door that led to dorm two hundred and seventeen. It had been exactly one and a half months since I laid eyes on Maddison, at least in person, and I was dying to touch her, to smell her, to feel her skin under my fingers.

I had just gotten her before she was gone again, and God, I

would never stop her from going after what she wanted, but I'd be lying if I said that the separation wasn't torture.

That was why I was here today. It wasn't planned. I have exams to study for and graduation to prepare for, and I knew that Maddison was just as busy. But none of that mattered. I needed to see her.

She opened the door with a pencil dangling between her teeth and her brow was still scrunched in concentration from whatever she was working on. She didn't even look up from the textbook in her hand as she pulled the door open and turned to walk back in the room.

"I hope you didn't get Chinese food." She turned the page as I stepped into her small space. "I've been craving it like crazy, but it makes me so homesick."

I couldn't help staring at her ass as she walked back toward her twin bed. She was wearing a pair of shorts—the tiniest scrap of fabric, and I almost fell to my knees at the way the curve of her ass was on display.

"How homesick are you exactly?"

She spun toward me so quickly the pencil flew through her mouth, and I had to duck to avoid a stab wound. She didn't answer my question. She just stared at me for a moment—one, two, three. I could feel my heart pounding in my chest as I counted the seconds that laid between us.

Her textbook left her hands at the count of five.

Her feet pushed her into motion at six.

Her body hit mine at the count of seven.

And just like that, in eight tiny seconds, I felt like I was breathing clearer than I had in months.

"What are you doing here?" Her words were muffled as she buried her face into my neck.

"I missed you." I shrugged my shoulders like it was no big

deal that I had just traveled over twelve hours to see my girlfriend of three months because I missed her.

She laughed, the sound bubbling out of her, and it was weird how attracted I was to it—that one simple sound.

"I cannot believe you're here." She pulled back from me and stared up at my face as if she was trying to take every single inch of me in. "I've missed you so much."

I couldn't stop myself as I leaned down and kissed her. Her lips felt softer somehow, her kiss more desperate than I remember, and I even though I didn't realize how badly, I needed that kiss from her as much as she needed it from me.

My fingers roamed over the edge of her t-shirt, and she laughed against my mouth. "My roommate should be back any minute with lunch."

I peppered kiss after kiss against her mouth as she spoke. I wasn't ready to stop.

"Shhh." I pressed my finger to her lips. "She won't even notice me."

She smiled, and I loved her carefree she looked—how much weight had been lifted off her. "Trust me when I tell you that she'll notice you."

I took a step toward her and forced her closer to her bed. "Are you saying I'm hot?" I wiggled my eyebrows as she laughed.

"All I'm saying is that you're hard to miss." She rolled her eyes, and I took one more step.

"Because I'm hot."

"No." She shook her head before looking back to see how much space was between us and her mattress. "Because you've got a really big head."

"You know." I put my hands on her hips and stopped our pace. "I knew it the moment I met you."

"Knew what? That you were full of it?"

"No." I smiled down at the girl I had been falling for far too easily. "That you were going to fall in love with me."

She sucked in a tiny little breath before she tried to laugh it off. "Is this going to be another story that you tell our children? How the princess fell so easily in love with the prince, and they lived happily ever after?"

"No." I shook my head and ran my tongue over my dry lips. "This is a different story."

"Oh yea?" She cocked her head to the side with the softest smile on her face, and I knew without a doubt that I may not have been the guy Maddison had always dreamed about, but I would always be everything she needed. "What's this story about then?"

"This is the story of how the big strong handsome prince charming—" She rolled her eyes again, but I kept going. "—fell irrevocably in love with the girl."

She blinked up with me, and I knew without her saying a word that she had fallen as easily as I had.

"I thought you weren't a prince charming." She ran her fingers through my hair and pulled my face closer to hers as she stood on her tip toes.

I wasn't a prince charming. Definitely not that kind of prince charming she had always had in mind, but for her, I'd be anything she wanted me to be.

"Turns out I was wrong."

ACKNOWLEDGMENTS

To every reader, blogger, and bookstagrammer who takes a chance on me and my books, thank you so much. It means more to me than you will ever know. Thank you!

To Hubie, I feel like you should probably be tired of me acknowledging you by now so I'm not going to talk about how supportive you are or how amazing of a father you are or how you have made so many sacrifices to help me follow my dreams. I just want you to know that you are so incredibly hot. Like the hottest. God, I could stare at you all day.

To my family, THANK YOU.

Thank you Becca for helping craft my story and for believing in me even when I don't. You are one of the best things about this little book world of ours.

Thank you to my amazing editor, Ellie McLove. You're the absolute tits.

To Regina Wamba, thank you for your brilliant mind and always knowing what I want even when I don't know how to say it.

To Linda, thank you for everything you do.